"May I kiss you, Emily?"

"I'm not sure that would be proper, Adam."

"We are friends."

"Yes. Yes, we are."

"Maybe we're a little more than friends."

"Maybe."

"We might become much more than friends."

"The contract I signed gave us six months to make a decision about that."

"Oh, yes. The escape clause." Adam smiled. "I believe the Thompson brothers did mention that."

"You know I didn't like you much when I first met you?"

"Yes, I know that." He leaned closer. His warm breath caressed her face. "I wasn't overly fond of you, either."

I should say no. I should—I really should say no. She fought a losing battle with her decorum. "You may kiss me, Adam."

M. J. CONNER is the pen name for sisters Mildred Colvin and Jean Norval. Mildred Colvin is a native Missourian with three children, one son-in-law, and two grandchildren. She and her husband spent most of their married life providing a home for foster children but now enjoy baby-sitting the grandchildren. Mildred writes inspirational romance novels because in them the truth of God's presence, even in the midst of trouble, can be portrayed. Her desire is to continue writing stories that uplift and encourage.

Jean Norval, mother of one daughter and two sons, and grandmother to five boys and two girls, lived in Missouri most of her life. She loved books, whether reading or writing them. She and her husband were active in a small community church where she enjoyed the Bible discussions in the Sunday school class. She believed and tried to portray in her stories that we all are incomplete without God.

Books by M. J. Conner

HEARTSONG PRESENTS
HP435—Circle of Vengeance

Don't miss out on any of our super romances. Write to us at the following address for information on our newest releases and club information.

Heartsong Presents Readers' Service
PO Box 721
Uhrichsville, OH 44683

Or visit www.heartsongpresents.com

Escape to Sanctuary

M. J. Conner

Heartsong Presents

In memory of Jean Norval, coauthor of *Escape to Sanctuary*, who on February 16, 2004, went to be with the Savior whom she loved and served.

Jean had only begun to see the encouragement her writing brought to others when she was diagnosed with terminal cancer on January 16, 2004. Two days later, Jean wrote, "Help me to stay strong! I think my witness, whether I live or whether I die, can touch someone else." Her illness was brief as she continued to write and to speak, confident in her faith and focused on her witness to others. Her writing lives on today, bringing her readers a message of the eternal "escape to sanctuary."

A note from the Author:
I love to hear from my readers! You may correspond with me by writing:

M. J. Conner
Author Relations
PO Box 719
Uhrichsville, OH 44683

ISBN 1-59310-526-6

ESCAPE TO SANCTUARY

one

"Adam needs a wife." Ike Thompson looked across the supper table at his younger brother. "And I been thinking we should help him get one."

"You mean a mail-order bride?" Lewis squeezed the hand of the plump young woman seated at his right. "Like my Kirsten?"

"That's exactly what I been thinking," Ike said. "Yessir, old Adam needs a good woman."

"You got no call to be interfering in Adam Jacobs's life," Ike's wife, Bertha, said.

"Now, Bertie, we wouldn't be interfering." Ike grinned. "We'd just be helping out a friend."

Bertha mashed a piece of potato with her fork and shoved it into the mouth of the chubby toddler on her lap. "Adam don't want your help."

"Just a minute, Bertha." Lewis rubbed the back of his neck. "Me and Adam have been best friends since we wasn't much older than Tad there. I think Ike's right. We should help him out." He smiled at his wife. "I recollect I was balkier than a calf facing a hot branding iron when Clyde Simms suggested I answer that ad in the magazine for a mail-order bride. An' just look how good it turned out."

"You're not Adam Jacobs." Bertha persisted in her opposition. "Gertrude hurt Adam real bad. My ma always said, once burned, twice shy."

5

"Aw, Bertie, that was almost a year ago. It's time Adam got over that redheaded Jezebel."

"Ike's right about that," Lewis interjected. "Adam's lucky Gertrude—or Trudy as she called herself—took off 'fore they was married 'stead of after."

"It's our Christian duty to help a brother in need." Ike slapped the table with his open hand. "And that's what we're a-gonna do. Lewis, you get the writing paper and an envelope. We'll compose a letter that will get our friend a good wife. Kirsten, you write a pretty hand. Me and Lewis will tell you what to say and you set it down."

Kirsten took the pencil and tablet from her husband. Lewis sat back down beside her and draped an arm across the back of her chair. "Okay, honey, here's what you write. Prosperous Montana rancher in his midtwenties seeks wife."

"Better put in that he's looking for a Christian wife." Ike leaned across the table. "That's real important."

"Yeah, 'tis." Lewis rubbed the back of his neck. "And I reckon we better leave out that prosperous part. We don't want a gold digger answering this ad."

"Why don't we write something like this," Kirsten said. "Christian rancher in his midtwenties seeking wife. She must be a devout Christian woman between the ages of sixteen and twenty-four, not afraid of hard work, and willing to resettle in Montana."

"That sounds real good, honey." Lewis gave his bride an affectionate squeeze.

"I ain't getting involved in this." Bertha snorted. "But I can tell you right now, Adam Jacobs ain't gonna cotton to no sixteen-year-old girl."

"Now, Bertie, you don't know that." Ike glanced from his young sister-in-law to his wife then back again. "Maybe you'd best make that nineteen instead of sixteen, Kirsten."

Kirsten marked through what she had written and chewed on the end of the pencil for a moment before putting pen to paper. "Between the ages of nineteen and twenty-four." She looked up. "Does that sound better to you, Bertha?"

"Humph!" Bertha stood up, set the baby on Ike's knee, and began to clear the table. "I can tell you one thing for certain. No matter how you word that ad, Adam Jacobs is gonna be madder than a wet hen when a strange woman shows up on his doorstep."

&

The sun at the twelve o'clock position announced dinnertime even before the ringing of the farmhouse dinner bell brought the rakes and mowers to a standstill.

Adam Jacobs stepped down from the bare metal mower seat. As he stretched to release the kinks in his sore arms and back, his gaze swept over the mown field with its neat windrows of felled grass. The hay should be ready to stack tomorrow. He felt the satisfaction of a job well done.

Turning, he gazed across an expanse of tall, undulating grass to a simple four-room house surrounded by a plain board fence and backed by large barns, corrals, and sheds. The roses his mother had planted were a splash of red against the fence. He had grown to manhood there. Now it was his older brother John's home.

He looked some six hundred feet to his left. Whatever good spirits Adam felt over the morning's work vanished at the sight of his one-room unpainted cabin and outhouse sitting alone on the prairie.

"Hey, Adam!" John hollered. "You ready to eat?"

Adam unhitched the horses and led them to the shade. After they were watered and staked out to graze beside John's and the Thompson brothers' teams, the four men walked toward the house.

"We should have your hay put up by the end of the week," Ike said.

John nodded. "Should be able to move into your fields Monday morning."

"If it doesn't rain." Adam scowled at the cloudless blue sky.

Lewis gave a good-natured slap to Adam's shoulder. "It ain't gonna rain before we get the hay put up. Where's your faith, man?"

"I've got faith." Adam shrugged his friend's hand from his shoulder. "Faith that anything bad that can happen, will."

"That ain't so, Adam." Lewis shook his head. "There's lots of good in this world. All you gotta do is look around you."

"I'm looking." Adam turned his head toward the small cabin sitting alone on the prairie. "And I don't see anything good."

The other men made a halfhearted attempt at conversation, but Adam's foul mood cast a pall over the group, and the remainder of their walk was made in silence.

Bertha stood on the back porch with an armful of towels. "Get cleaned up before you come in the house." She laid the towels on the washstand beside a steaming basin of water. "Your dinner is waiting. Don't tarry or everything will be cold."

The screen door squealed and slammed behind her as she went back inside.

After the men washed up, they sat down to eat. Several minutes later, Ike sopped up the last of the gravy on his plate with a piece of fresh bread. "You surely outdone yourselves today, ladies." He popped the morsel in his mouth. "These is mighty fine eats."

Ruth and Kirsten both smiled in acknowledgment of the compliment. Bertha grunted and continued to spoon mashed potatoes and gravy into baby Tad's mouth.

"One of these days, everything I've got will go to Tad and

his brothers." Ike leaned back in his chair. "It gives a man a sense of. . .of. . .immortality, I reckon you'd say, to know he's building something for the future. Why, when me and Lewis is dead and gone, there'll still be Thompsons farming this land. Ain't that right, Lewis?"

"Yessir, it surely is." Lewis speared a piece of fried chicken and deposited it on his plate. "There ain't nothing like having a good, God-fearing woman to share your life with. I didn't know how lonely I was till my Kirsten came to me."

He looked across at Adam sitting in his usual place at the old round oak table that had belonged to his mother. "You ever give any thought to getting married, Adam? I mean, since Trudy left."

Adam looked up from his plate. "No, I haven't, Lewis." His voice was level and flat. "I'm perfectly content the way I am."

"Well now, Adam, you know that ain't true." Ike put his two cents' worth in. "God never meant a man to live alone. That's why he created the woman to be his helpmeet."

Ruth set a piece of cherry pie in front of John. "Would anyone else care for pie?"

Both Thompson brothers nodded yes to the pie but were not deterred from their train of thought. "Trudy ain't worth moping over, Adam." Ike spoke around a mouthful of pie. "You oughta thank your lucky stars she left when she did."

"I'm not moping, Ike." Adam clenched his hands beneath the tablecloth. "But if I were, it would be my own business."

"Well, that's neither here nor there now," Lewis chimed in. "What you oughta do is send back East for a wife like I done."

Adam shoved his chair back and stood. "You order a saddle blanket, Lewis. Not a wife." He blurted the words before he thought them through.

Over Lewis's shoulder, he saw Kirsten's stricken face. "I'm sorry, ma'am. Truly I am. I meant no offense to you. But I don't want a wife, mail-order or any other kind. Now I'm going back to work." He turned and stalked out the door.

&

Two months later, the Thompson brothers were uncharacteristically quiet and ill at ease when they sat down across the table from Adam at the church's October fellowship dinner.

Lewis cleared his throat. "Adam, I reckon you haven't had a change of heart about that mail-order bride, have you?"

"I have not." Adam raised his head and looked directly into Lewis's eyes. "Look, Lewis. I've said it before, and I'll say it again. I don't want a bride—mail-order or otherwise."

If they hadn't been at a church dinner, he would have told Lewis exactly what he thought of a woman who would resort to answering an ad to find a husband. Instead, he continued his meal, shoving the food into his mouth with a vengeance and hoping the Thompson brothers would take the hint and go elsewhere to eat. They didn't.

"Adam, me and Lewis got something we need to tell you." Ike pulled at his collar. "Now don't go getting mad at us. We meant well. And when we found out how you felt about it, we tried to undo it. Honest, we did. But it was too late."

The brothers had the sheepish appearance of a couple of egg-sucking dogs caught in the act. A sense of foreboding crept over Adam. "Too late for what, Ike?"

"It ain't really as bad as it sounds." Ike's voice took on a cheerful note. "On account of Bertie made us put this clause in." He leaned forward. "Kind of like an escape clause, you might say. You got six months to decide if you want to keep her."

"Keep her!" Adam gripped the fork in his hand so tightly the handle bent. "Keep who, Ike?"

He looked slowly from one brother to the other, a feeling of dread churning his insides. "What have you done?"

"Now don't go getting all upset," Lewis said. "We was only

trying to help. And it ain't like it can't be undone."

"What can't be undone?" Adam watched the brothers wilt under his daggered stare. "What have you done?" he repeated.

"Well, you see, it's like this." Lewis took a swallow of water. "My Kirsten is a real jewel. We're expecting a little one in six months. There ain't nothing like having a family, Adam. And, well, me and you been friends since we was boys. I couldn't stand to see you so down in the mouth."

He rubbed the back of his neck. "I mean, you been moping around, and me and Ike decided you needed a good woman to take your mind off things. So seeing as how we had a little extra money, we sent for a bride for you."

"A bride!" Adam trembled with barely suppressed rage. "You had no right to stick your nose into my affairs."

"We know we didn't. And, well, we're right sorry we done it. But at the time, it seemed like a good idea." Ike reached into his pocket and pulled out a crumpled piece of paper. "This here telegram come for you last week."

When Adam refused to take it from his outstretched hand, Ike laid it on the table between them.

"If we weren't in church, I'd thrash the living daylights out of both of you."

"Well, we kinda thought you might feel that way." Ike's laugh sounded forced. "That's why we decided to tell you at church."

Lewis pushed back his chair and stood. "I reckon we'd best be getting on home, Ike." His gaze rested on Adam for a moment before sliding away. "Kirsten wasn't feeling too good, and Bertha stayed home with her. We wouldn't have come neither, but we thought we ought to tell you about your bride coming and all, so's you can pick her up. She'll be arriving at the depot tomorrow."

"Tomorrow!" The blood pounded in Adam's ears. "You

ordered her, Lewis Thompson. You pick her up."

"Well, I would. . ." Lewis and Ike edged toward the door. "But it wouldn't look proper, what with me being a married man and all. Besides, with my Kirsten feeling so puny, I can't see my way clear to leave her alone any more than's necessary."

As the door swung closed behind the brothers, Adam grabbed up the telegram and read a confirmation of what they had just told him. Tomorrow afternoon, a woman he hadn't asked for and didn't want would arrive at the train station expecting him to meet her.

Adam lurched from his chair and found his brother. "I'm going home, John."

"What's wrong?"

Too angry to speak, Adam thrust the telegram into his brother's hand.

He didn't look back as he crossed the room and closed the door behind him. What had Lewis and Ike been thinking? The talk was beginning to die down about him and Trudy. Now this! He knew what the main topic of conversation in Sanctuary would be for the next six months. Him. And this. . .this. . .girl the Thompson brothers had bought for him. Well, he for sure wasn't meeting her train tomorrow. For all he cared, she could sit in the train station till doomsday. As for the Thompson brothers. . .

He mounted his horse, Copper, and rode away from the church. Why couldn't they have just left well enough alone? Why couldn't everybody just leave him be?

two

Adam's anger on Sunday was nothing compared to the fury that roiled through him as he hitched the big draft horses to the wagon on Monday. It was spitting snow. He figured it would turn into a full-fledged blizzard before he got back home.

"Lewis should have been the one going out in bad weather to meet this girl. I have half a notion to leave her sitting in the station."

"It's not her fault, Adam." His brother had been listening to him fume for the last hour. "She accepted your offer in good faith."

"My offer!" Adam snorted. "I never offered her anything."

"She doesn't know that."

Adam checked the harness. "What kind of woman would answer an ad like that, John?"

"Maybe she's an orphan like Kirsten."

"Yeah, that's what I've been thinking. She's probably a sixteen-year-old kid." His shoulders slumped. "I'd rather take a beating than drive into Sanctuary today."

"Dad raised us to honor our commitments." John slapped Adam on the shoulder. "You can't leave her sitting in the depot."

"I know." Adam scowled. "I'll pick her up at the depot and drive her to Mrs. Carlyle's boardinghouse. I'll give her money to buy a ticket back to wherever she came from because that is the honorable thing to do. But I won't pretend to be happy about it."

John raised the lid of the box behind the seat and put two

folded blankets in the covered storage place. "We'll be praying for you."

"I'll be back before dark if I don't get caught in a blizzard and freeze to death on the way home." Adam swung up on the wagon seat.

He released the brake and drove out of the barnyard. The cold stung the exposed skin of his face as the gray horses plodded along. If he had ridden Copper, he would have made the trip in half the time. That's what he should have done. Ridden his saddle horse and let the girl get her luggage to the boardinghouse the best way she could.

An honorable man. "Yeah, and what's that going to get me? Frozen solid most likely. I just hope when they discover my lifeless remains come spring, Lewis Thompson knows he's responsible."

Lewis had been his best friend for as long as he could remember. In all those years, he had pulled some boneheaded stunts, but this was the worst thing he had ever done. Just because Lewis was happy being married to a silly kid didn't mean Adam would be.

Adam pulled his coat collar up around his neck. "If I was looking for a wife—which I'm not—I'd want a woman I could talk to. All Kirsten does is giggle and ask questions. I'd go crazy if I had to live with a woman like that. The sooner this girl is gone the better."

❧

Emily Foster made a halfhearted attempt to brush the soot from her threadbare coat. Bits and pieces of a Bible verse her mother always quoted about the ways of God being past understanding had been running through her mind ever since she boarded the train. She should remember all of it, but with her head pounding like this, she couldn't think. The past week was hazy and out of focus. The only thing that stood out clearly in her mind was her abduction.

Was it just one week ago that she had been hurrying along a dark New York City street? Fearful of every strange sound, she had kept her head bent low as she clutched her shabby coat close, although the worn garment provided little protection from the damp chill of the October night.

She walked on, placing one tired foot in front of the other. Her footfalls were now the only sound on the deserted street. Then she stumbled over a loose brick and looked up. That was when she saw a wavering light on the corner ahead. Quickly, she shrank back into the shadows, her heart thundering in her ears.

The thickening fog shrouded the covered hack and the two dark horses as they rounded the corner and rolled silently down the street toward her. If not for the feeble glow of the lanterns on the front of the hack, she wouldn't have seen them.

She shivered as they passed her without slowing. Not until the sinister vehicle rounded the corner, almost three-quarters of a city block away, did she dare catch her breath. Venturing from the shadows, she scurried on her way.

In the two weeks preceding that October evening, three girls from the Triangle Shirtwaist Company had disappeared. One day they had been there; the next day they were gone. Vanished. There were whispered rumors that they had been murdered. Killed because of their support of the ILGWU, the International Ladies Garment Workers Union.

Emily hadn't lost her life because of her outspoken support of the union, but that night she had lost her job. When her meager savings, the few dollars she had scrimped to save and put back against the day she could leave the city, were gone, Mrs. Riley would be only too happy to toss her few pitiful belongings into the street. How was she to survive the coming winter?

Please, Lord. Please don't let me perish in the streets. Please, Father...

A muffled sound intruded on her desperate prayer. She glanced over her shoulder and saw the hack had turned and now crept toward her from behind. With desperate eyes, she searched for a hiding place and found none. The hack drew up beside her. She quickened her steps. The shadowy form of a man leaped to the street.

Emily stifled a scream. With a burst of terror, she took flight, running for her life. She heard the pounding of footsteps behind her and knew her assailant was rapidly closing the gap. With every ounce of strength she could muster, she forced her tired limbs to carry her forward.

She could hear the man's quick breath behind her. The horse, too, kept pace. A dreamlike reality took shape as she gasped for air and willed herself forward. Then a heavy hand fell on her shoulder, and she knew it was over. Another man joined the first, and yet she fought but could not keep the rope from tightening around her wrists, tearing at her tender skin until it became raw and painful. Her prayer for deliverance seemed to go unanswered when the men grabbed her and dumped her, hog-tied, gagged, and blindfolded, on the floor of the hack.

She lay there for a long time, it seemed, until the hack stopped and one of the men dragged her into the cold night air, then jerked off her blindfold. They stood outside an old building she assumed had once been a hotel. After freeing her from the ropes that bound her, they forced her up a rickety staircase to a cold, drafty room and locked her inside. Still wearing her damp clothes, she huddled under a thin blanket on the unoccupied of two beds in the room and tried to make sense of what was happening to her. Why had these men taken her? Was it because of her support of the ILGWU?

Did they plan to kill her? The next morning, when the young girl who shared her room awoke, she introduced herself as Daisy. From this girl, who was little more than a child, Emily discovered what the two men had planned for her.

The men were white slavers. That very morning, Daisy said, the girls who were being held in this building would be sold to brothels.

Emily began to pray in earnest. Remembering the Old Testament account of Daniel and his three friends, she determined to do nothing that would dishonor God. If these men killed her, so be it. She would die honorably.

When a man called Buck brought breakfast, she refused to eat it. When he returned later with an armful of tawdry costumes, Emily refused to wear the skimpy dresses. When he brought a woman to style her hair and paint her face, Emily refused again and began to pray aloud. The more they tried to force her to comply, the more fervent her prayers became. Then Buck hit her, and she began to pray for the salvation of her captors. The man stormed from the room after declaring he would happily pay someone to take her off his hands.

A marriage broker named Smith offered her an unexpected avenue of escape. He told her if she accepted his offer, she would be going to Montana as a mail-order bride. Although she had no intentions of marrying any man, Emily desperately wanted to go west and, thanking God for this escape, gladly signed a contract agreeing to marry a man named Adam Jacobs.

Mr. Smith guarded her every move but allowed her to pick up her things from Mrs. Riley's before he put her on the train that would eventually take her to Montana. Sanctuary, Montana. She prayed it would be the place of safety its name implied.

When the train slowed, Emily stood. The sudden movement caused a spell of dizziness that blurred her vision. She gripped the back of the seat in front of her until she regained her balance.

Despite her fragile appearance, Emily was rarely ill. The combination of months of malnutrition and the night she spent in the drafty, frigid room in the old hotel had resulted in a cold that seemed to have settled in her lungs. After the dizziness passed, she managed to reach into the overhead compartment and pull her bag down.

Most of last night and all of today, she had chilled. Thankfully, the trip was over. With food and rest, she should regain her strength. But first she had to face this man—this Adam Jacobs. Surely, after she told him that as soon as she found work, she planned to return the money he had spent on her train fare, he would be kind enough to direct her to a boardinghouse.

The train screeched to a halt. Emily felt as though she struggled through fog as she made her way down the aisle. She stepped off the train into six inches of fresh snow. The sky in early afternoon was twilight gray. Huge snowflakes danced through the frigid air and settled on her eyelashes. Pulling her coat closer, she struggled up two steps and across the dock of the train station. She pushed open the heavy door and walked into a small, deserted room. She assumed the stationmaster must be outside helping the engineer and conductor take on fuel.

A potbellied stove stood to one side of the room beside a long bench. Emily dropped her bag on the end of the bench nearest the stove and sat down beside it. Her eyelids drooped, then drifted shut.

She jerked awake when the train whistle sounded. Through a feverish haze, she saw black smoke puff from the smokestack of the engine. The whistle once more sounded. The train began to move slowly at first, then faster and faster until, with a rumble that shook the building, it moved out of sight.

In the sudden silence, Emily heard a door slam in the back of the building. She turned toward the sound and caught a glimpse of movement outside the window across from her. Through the snow, which was now a lacy curtain, she saw a wagon and two huge horses. A man swung down from the wagon seat and headed for the corner of the building, where he momentarily disappeared. Was this Mr. Jacobs?

The door swung open, then slammed closed behind him. He was tall and husky, the lower half of his face covered by an unkempt beard. His dark eyes flashed fire when his gaze came to rest on her.

"Are you the mail-order bride?" His voice sounded as angry as his eyes looked.

Emily shrunk back against the bench and nodded.

"Hey, Adam, what brings you into town on a day like this?"

Emily's gaze followed that of the stranger, and they both looked at the gangly young man who had entered the room from the back.

"It wasn't my idea," the big man snapped. "I'm picking her up for Lewis." He gestured toward Emily. "But she isn't staying. I'm taking her over to Mrs. Carlyle. Next train comes through heading east, I want her on it."

How dare this man—this Adam Jacobs—speak of her in such a disparaging manner. "I'm not going back," she said.

Both men looked at her. Adam Jacobs scowled as his words cut through the air. "I have no intention of marrying you."

"Now that I have met you, Mr. Jacobs," Emily retorted, "I wouldn't entertain the idea of matrimony if you were the last man on earth."

She broke into a spasm of coughing that left her weak.

"This is just great," the big man said. "On top of everything else, she's sick. I guess I'll have to take her to Doc Brown."

"Can't," the lanky man said, curiosity brightening his eyes. "Doc left town at noon. Simmonses' baby got the croup. Snowin' like it is, he'll probably be out there a spell."

"I can't leave her at Mrs. Carlyle's." He frowned at her as if it was her fault she was sick. "She might die over there with no one to see about her."

"I reckon you'll have to take her to Ruth."

"I don't see as I have any choice unless I want her death on my conscience. I better throw her luggage in the wagon and get on home."

"She don't have anything," the other man said, "except that one bag."

The man's brown-eyed gaze came to rest on Emily. His stormy expression revealed his anger. "Come on. I better get you to Ruth before it gets any worse out."

Emily had no intention of going anywhere with this arrogant man. She stood to tell him so and the room shifted and began to spin. The two men, the station, everything around her receded into the distance. She felt herself falling and was vaguely aware of someone catching her as she plunged into the darkness.

three

Adam looked down at the slight form lying on the wagon seat beside him. Tom had gone to his living quarters in the back of the station and returned with the pillow that cushioned the young woman's head. He'd also brought an extra blanket, which Adam tucked around her along with the two that John had put in the wagon. He pulled off his glove and rested his fingers against her throat. Her heartbeat seemed strong, but she was burning up with fever.

He put his glove back on and adjusted the blankets until she was completely covered except for a small air space in front of her face.

It couldn't have been much later than two o'clock, but already it was almost dark. The wind whipped the snow into drifts that made it rough going for the horses. Gusts shaped and reshaped the white landscape until familiar landmarks disappeared or were unrecognizable.

Adam was sure the girl had pneumonia. He remembered how it had been two years ago when Ruth and his mother got pneumonia. Ruth survived. Mom didn't. The girl on the seat beside him was small and frail. As soon as she was well, he would take her back to town and put her on the train headed east. He tried not to think that she might not get well.

"I'm not going anywhere." The young woman's words had barely registered back at the train station. She had spunk. He'd have to give her that. As sick as she was, he'd detected an independent streak in her. Well, independent and spunky as she might be, as soon as she was able to travel, she was

21

going back where she came from. The West was no place for a sickly female.

Adam checked the girl's pulse once more. The anger that had been smoldering under the surface of his worry for the young woman rekindled to burn brightly in his chest. His resentment focused on his friend. Lewis should be the one out in the storm with a sick girl, struggling to make it home, wondering if she would die before he got her to shelter. If Lewis hadn't stuck his nose where it didn't belong, this girl would be safe and secure.

A few minutes later, the horses came to a standstill beside his brother's porch. Adam yelled for John before jumping down from the high wagon seat. The door swung open, spilling forth welcome light as Adam scooped the blanket-swaddled bundle from the seat.

Warmth surrounded him when he carried the girl into Ruth's kitchen. John pushed the door closed behind them. "She's sick, Ruth. Where can I lay her down?"

"Just a minute." Ruth filled a warming pan with hot coals and hurried into the bedroom that Adam and John had shared when they were boys. "I thought you would be sleeping here tonight," she called over her shoulder, "so I left the door open."

While his sister-in-law turned back the bedclothes and warmed the cold sheets, Adam handed the girl to John. "I need to take care of the horses," he said. "I'll explain everything when I come back in."

Adam set the girl's bag inside the door before taking the team and wagon to the barn. After the horses were fed and watered, he saw to the cows in the corral, then went back inside.

After he warmed up a bit, Adam ventured as far as the bedroom doorway and looked inside. The girl was still unconscious. The covers were drawn up to her chin. She looked even frailer than he remembered. Black eyelashes cast a shadow on her small, pinched face. Except for the unnatural redness of her cheeks, her skin was stark white. The room reeked of camphor.

"Do you think she'll make it?" Adam whispered.

"I've done all I know to do. The rest is in God's hands." Ruth adjusted the quilt over the slight body. "Do you know where she was before she came here, Adam?"

"Somewhere back East, I guess." He shrugged. "I don't even know her name."

"It's on her bag. Her name is Emily Foster, and she came from New York City." Ruth moved closer to the bed. "But that isn't what I meant. I want to show you something."

She lifted the girl's arms from under the covers. "I noticed this when I was getting her ready for bed." She pushed the gown's long sleeves up. "What do you think made these marks on her wrists?"

Adam moved closer to the bed. His stomach twisted when he realized what had caused the marks. "Those are rope burns."

"That's what John thought." Ruth sighed. "Poor little thing!"

Adam took a last look at the girl's pale face before joining his brother in the kitchen. He poured a cup of coffee and sat down at the table.

John looked up from the magazine he was reading. "Ruth show you the gal's wrists?"

Adam nodded. "She must have put up quite a struggle."

John bent his head over his magazine. Adam sipped coffee and thought about the girl in the bedroom. The marks on her wrists weren't that old. Maybe she hadn't come from such a safe place after all.

John closed the magazine and laid it aside. "You explain things to her?"

"I told her I wasn't going to marry her." Recalling his rudeness, Adam blushed. "I suppose I should have been kinder about it, but I was really angry by the time I got to the depot."

"You tell her about Ike and Lewis?"

"Not exactly." Thinking how he talked to Tom about the girl instead of directly to her shamed him. "I wonder who did that to her, John."

"Hard to say." John went to the stove and refilled his cup. "There's lots of evil in the world."

She had felt light as thistle down when he carried her to the wagon. Adam looked into the depths of his coffee cup. She was so frail. How could anyone hurt her?

After a thoughtful silence, he said, "Maybe that's why she answered Lewis's ad. Maybe she's running away from someone."

"Could be." John sipped his coffee.

"I told her I was sending her back where she came from."

"What did she say?"

"She said she wasn't going."

John studied his brother's face. "What are you going to do about her?"

"I don't know." Adam thought of the rope burns on the girl's delicate wrists. Glancing toward the open bedroom door, he saw Ruth sitting in a rocking chair beside the bed. "But she can't go back."

"She's a sick girl," John said.

Adam didn't want to think that the girl might die, but he knew it was a possibility. "As soon as the storm dies down, I'll ride into town and bring Doc Brown out."

Ruth walked into the kitchen. She took a tin of carbolic salve and a roll of white bandages from the cabinet drawer. "I'm going to bandage her wrists. Then I thought I might try to get a bit of broth down her. Which reminds me. . ."

She left the bandages and salve on the cabinet and took a

heavy earthenware bowl from the shelf. "You haven't eaten since breakfast, Adam. You must be starved."

Adam hadn't thought about food until Ruth removed the lid from the large pot on the back of the stove. The smell of simmering beef and vegetables caused his stomach to growl. Ruth placed the steaming bowl in front of him, along with two huge squares of corn bread, before retrieving her bandages and returning to the bedroom.

He was finishing his second bowl of the savory soup when Ruth returned to strain some broth into a mug. "I don't feel comfortable leaving Miss Foster alone. John, would you and Adam set up the folding cot for me? I'll sleep in there tonight."

While the two men did as she requested, Ruth fed her patient sips of broth. She still wasn't aware of her surroundings as far as Adam could tell, but she swallowed the broth.

"She seems to have a little more color in her face," he said.

Ruth set the empty cup on the bedside table and lay the back of her hand against the young woman's forehead. "It may be the fever. She's burning up."

"Don't we have a bottle of the medicine Doc left when Mom was sick?" John asked.

"It's in the cabinet," Ruth said. "Would you get it for me?"

While John was gone, Adam stood looking down at the girl. As far as he knew, Doc Brown had never been to medical school. Instead, as with most pioneer doctors, he had studied medicine with an acting physician. Elias Brown was a good man, but he just didn't have the knowledge to be obtained in a university.

Adam knew if he had been allowed to finish school, he might have been able to do something to help the girl. As it was, he was helpless. He felt his anger rising at what he considered one of the greatest injustices of his life—the theft of his dreams.

John returned with the sealed bottle and a tablespoon. Ruth poured a dose of elixir, which Adam suspected was mostly whiskey, and gave it to the young woman. She choked a bit on the fiery liquid but managed to get it down.

"We need to pray for her healing." Ruth reached a hand to John. "Will you join me? You and Adam."

John clasped his wife's hand. Adam shook his head. "I'd better go see to the cows."

Adam could hear Ruth praying as he shrugged into his coat then pulled on a stocking cap and heavy gloves. John was praying by the time Adam wrapped the blue muffler around his neck, the one his mother had knitted for him the year before she died.

Adam opened the door and stepped into the driving snow. The wind whistling around the corner of the house took his breath. He made his way down the steps then grasped the rope tied to the porch post. The storm had increased in intensity in the last couple of hours. Lucky he made it home when he did. Otherwise, they might have been lost in the blizzard.

He thought of John and Ruth praying for the sick girl. They should have learned by now that prayer was useless. It hadn't saved their unborn child. It hadn't saved Mom. The darkness engulfed him as he plunged into the howling storm.

Struggling through knee-deep snow, buffeted by wind gusts that almost took him down, Adam clung to the rope and pushed on until he bumped into the solid bulk of the barn. Once inside, he lit the lantern. Taking the long black-snake whip from the wall, he slipped through a side door into the corral. Cracking the whip over the cows' backs, he forced them to run around the corral.

Back inside the barn, he checked on the horses and calves, then he blew out the flame in the lantern and let himself back into the cold.

Inside his brother's house, divested of his outer garments, he sat at the kitchen table drinking hot coffee. "I'd say it's not more than twenty degrees below zero out there, and the wind is ferocious."

John grinned at his younger brother. "Since Ruth's sleeping on the cot, you can bunk with me tonight."

Adam shook his head. "No, thank you. As I remember it, you hog the covers."

John shrugged. "Your only other choice is the couch or a pallet in front of the fireplace."

Adam knew they would have to be up periodically to rouse the cattle. His house was too far from the barns and the corral. In bad weather, he always slept in the bed that the mail-order bride was now occupying.

"I'll take a pallet," he said. Though he knew it wouldn't be as comfortable as the bed, it was better than the couch. "How's she doing?"

John shook his head. "Ruth has done all she knows to do. Her life is in God's hands now."

Adam grunted. "In that case, we might as well figure on burying her."

A pained expression crossed John's face. "You know better than that, little brother."

Adam shrugged. At one time, he had believed the same as John. But with each loss in their lives, believing had become harder and harder.

A few moments of silence hung heavy between the two men. "I think I'll go to bed," Adam said. "It's going to be a long night."

four

Emily floated in a black world, relieved only by occasional periods of swirling gray mist. During those moments of semiconsciousness, she was aware of gentle hands bathing her burning body. She heard a soft, feminine voice urging her to swallow the broth that trickled down her throat. Two voices—a man and a woman—prayed over her. She drifted back into the darkness.

Flames erupted in the velvety blackness. A crimson and gold inferno. Through the flames, she could see the outline of the home she shared with her parents.

"No! Please, God, no!" When she screamed, the flames seared her throat. Dry coughs shook her body. She struggled to breathe.

"It's all right," the gentle voice spoke. "Swallow this."

The liquid scalded her raw throat as it burned its way into her stomach. The gentle hands bathed her face and throat with cool water. An arm slipped around her shoulders and lifted her from the pillow. The rim of a glass pressed against her lips. She drank. She heard the gentle voice whispering her name in a prayer. The fire receded into the darkness, and she slept.

Emily ran through the wispy fog until her lungs felt as though they would burst. "Deliver me from evil, Father." As she gasped the frantic prayer, a rough hand closed around her arm. She cried out, "I will fear no evil; for Thou art with me."

She struggled to free her wrists until the ropes that bound her were slippery with her own blood.

28

Adam removed his boots and lay down on the pallet fully clothed. Knowing he would have to get up in a couple of hours, he slept lightly. The girl's screams woke him.

"Is she all right?" He arrived at the bedroom door two steps behind his brother.

"She's delirious," Ruth replied. "I gave her another dose of medicine." She wrung out the washcloth and pressed it to the girl's throat, then bathed her face. "She's burning up with fever. John, would you bring me a glass of cold water?"

Adam stepped aside to let John pass. He watched while his brother slipped an arm around the girl's shoulder and lifted her so she could drink. It was so reminiscent of his mother's final illness that Adam had to turn away. He pulled on his boots and outer garments and went to the barn. When he came back into the house, John and Ruth had gone to bed. Bathed in the dim glow of lamplight, the girl was deathly still. Adam stood in the kitchen until he detected a slight twitching of her eyelids, then he went to bed.

It was early morning before he heard the girl again. This time he stood at the bedroom door watching as she thrashed around, tearing at the bandages on her wrists.

With John's help, Ruth managed to calm her.

That evening the wind died down. Sometime after midnight, the snow ended. Early the following morning, Adam saddled Copper and rode into town after the doctor. It was late afternoon when they returned.

"How is she?" Adam asked when Ruth met them at the door.

"About the same." Ruth took the doctor's coat and hat. "She has a dry cough and a fever, though she may not be as hot as she was yesterday. She mumbles quite a bit, but I can't make head nor tail of what she's saying."

The doctor held his hands over the kitchen range to warm them. "Has she been able to take nourishment?"

"I've given her oatmeal gruel, beef broth, and warm tea."

"Good. Our first task is to bring down the fever." The doctor rubbed his hands together. "I believe I'm sufficiently warmed to see my patient."

"I'll take care of the horses." Adam pulled his cap down over his ears and buttoned his coat.

"John is in the barn," Ruth said as he pulled the door closed behind him.

After supper, Adam returned to his own house. Doc Brown spent the night at Emily's bedside. He piled quilts on her, then mixed a potion of drugs and gave her a medicine dropper full each hour. Shortly after midnight, her fever broke. The next morning, the sun came up, and Adam took the doctor back to town.

⁂

When Emily awoke, a banner of midmorning sunlight stretched across the bed. She had a hazy memory of arriving at the train station and after that nothing. She tried to push herself up on the pillows but hadn't the strength.

A tall, blond woman moved into her line of vision. "You're awake."

She recognized the soft, gentle voice. She wanted to ask questions, but the inside of her mouth was dry as a desert. "Water." She managed to croak. "Please."

The water was ice cold. She drained the glass the woman held to her lips. "Thank you."

She struggled to stay awake but couldn't force her eyelids to remain open.

When next she awoke, the blond woman was sitting in a chair next to the bed. She laid her knitting aside and stood to lean over Emily. "Are you hungry?"

She was hungry, but she had a more immediate problem. "I need to use the necessary."

"I'm not surprised." The woman laughed. "Doc gave you a massive dose of Epsom salts. Here, let me help you."

Despite her embarrassment, Emily had no choice but to let the woman help her to the chamber pot then back into bed. "My name is Ruth Jacobs," the blond woman said as she tucked the quilts around Emily.

"Where am I?" Emily asked. "How did I get here?"

"Adam brought you. This is my home. Mine and my husband John's." She straightened. "Adam Jacobs is my brother-in-law."

Emily recalled the big lout who had met her at the train. "I remember Mr. Jacobs," she said.

"Adam can be quite memorable," Ruth said with a cheerful smile. "Now I am going to get you something to eat."

Emily was so weak. Even that small amount of conversation had tired her. She dozed until Ruth returned with an invalid's tray. Dry toast and hot tea had never tasted so good, but she couldn't finish it. Chewing and swallowing took too much effort and brought on a fit of coughing anyway.

After the tray had been removed, Ruth resumed her seat beside the bed. Emily had dozens of questions but lacked the strength to ask them. Ruth's gentle humming hastened her sleep.

⁂

The girl was asleep when Adam and John came in at noon. When they asked how she was doing, Ruth said she was much better. "She woke and asked for a glass of water this morning. Her temperature is normal. After she rests a week or so, she should be good as new."

"How soon do you think she should be able to leave?" Adam looked up from his meal with a scowl.

"She can stay here until she is strong enough to leave," John said.

"She has nowhere else to go." Ruth sighed. "Poor girl! She's little more than a child."

"That's another thing. Lewis had no business enticing a young girl to come way out here." Adam laid down his fork. "A law was passed in June making it illegal to transport a woman across the state line for immoral purposes. I think they call it the Mann Act. Lewis was probably breaking that law."

"He didn't bring her out here for immoral purposes, Adam." John glanced at his younger brother. "He expected you to marry her."

"Yeah! Well, he should have better sense than to take something like that for granted."

"Lewis loves you, Adam." Ruth pushed a pea around on her plate. "He meant well."

"She's not my responsibility. Lewis sent for her. Lewis can find her a home."

"She's not a kitten to be given away," Ruth said.

"Well, she can't stay here."

Adam had been so afraid the mail-order bride would die. This morning when the doctor said the girl's fever had broken and she would recover, he had been weak with relief. Then he began to get angry all over again. Not at the girl. He figured she'd done what she had to do. But Lewis. That was a different story. Lewis didn't have a lick of sense. Lewis Thompson had been his best friend for as long as he could remember. Well, not anymore. His friendship with Lewis Thompson had ended the day Lewis and Ike sent that ad.

That afternoon, John and Adam caught up on chores in the barn that had been let go during the busy harvest season. They mended harnesses, and Adam groused. They mucked out stalls, and he complained. They cleaned the tack room, and he griped. Finally, John sat down on an upturned barrel.

"All right," he said. "What's bothering you? You're as cantankerous as a lop-eared mule with a bellyache."

"Nothing is bothering me." Adam kicked at a bale of twine. "Why should anything be bothering me? My former best friend dumps a sick girl off on me. I can't send her back because somebody where she came from evidently hurt her. I can't keep her because. . .because I don't want her. I don't want to be responsible for anyone. But I feel responsible for her. So as soon as she's well, I have to find her a home. Why should anything be bothering me? I have no problems. I'm happy as a lark."

"Does this have anything to do with Gertrude Phillips?"

"Trudy is gone, John. And as far as I'm concerned, it's good riddance." Adam slammed his fist into the wall. "Why is it so hard for everybody to believe that?"

"Maybe because ever since she left, you've acted like a bear with a sore paw."

"Yeah, well, it's a little irritating to have everyone feeling sorry for me. Every time I go to town, I hear people whispering behind my back. 'Poor Adam. Gertrude broke his heart. Ain't it a shame?'" Adam could feel the heat climbing up his neck at the very thought.

"I don't need people feeling sorry for me. And I sure as the world don't need Lewis Thompson buying me a wife. If I want a woman, I'm perfectly capable of finding my own." He sent the ball of twine reeling across the tack room with a tap of his boot. "If I wanted to raise kids, I'd get married and have my own; I for sure wouldn't marry one."

John shrugged his shoulders and went back to cleaning the tack room. Adam stomped off and began mucking out stalls with a vengeance.

That night when they went in for supper, the mail-order bride was asleep, but Ruth said she had been awake that afternoon. Adam was relieved to hear she had managed to eat some solid food. She woke again before he left to go to his own house. Ruth closed the door when she went in to tend her, so he didn't see her that night.

⋅ৰ

The next morning, Ruth brought a tray with a steaming bowl of oatmeal, a cup of hot tea, and two slices of toasted home-made bread coated with apple butter. She ate every bite, then leaned back against the pillows.

"Thank you, Mrs. Jacobs."

"You are welcome." Ruth smiled as she removed the tray. "But please, call me Ruth."

"My name is Emily." She extended a slender hand. "I'm pleased to make your acquaintance, Ruth."

Ruth briefly grasped the girl's hand. "I can tell you are feeling better."

"Yes, much better, thanks to you. The breakfast was delicious."

"You haven't eaten anything substantial for some time. I should imagine anything would taste good to you."

"I must have been here since Monday evening." Emily looked toward the frost-painted window. "There was a blizzard, wasn't there?"

"Yes, you slept through it."

"I heard the wind howling around the house." Emily's brow knitted in concentration. "There was a doctor here, wasn't there?"

"Yes." Ruth set the tray on the table. "That was Doc Brown. He spent Tuesday night here. Adam rode into town Tuesday morning and brought him to see you."

Emily thought of the angry man she had met at the train

station. "Mr. Jacobs did?"

"Adam has been very worried about you. We all have."
Ruth picked up the tray. "Do you feel like sitting in a chair
for a few minutes?"

"Yes. I would like that."

"All right." Ruth smiled. "I'll take your tray to the kitchen,
then I'll help you up."

"Thank you," Emily murmured. She knew the sooner she
got up, the sooner she would regain her strength. But her
eyelids felt heavy. Despite her determination to stay awake,
her eyes closed.

When she woke again, Ruth was sitting in the rocking
chair next to the bed, knitting. "What time is it?"

"A few minutes past one o'clock." Ruth laid the yarn aside.
"Would you like to use the chamber pot?"

Emily nodded. "Please."

After Ruth helped her back into bed, she lay weak and
trembling against the pillows. Frustration brought tears to
her eyes. She couldn't impose on the kindness of strangers
forever. She must regain her strength.

Ruth left the room and returned a few minutes later
with a tray. Emily wasn't hungry, but she forced herself to
eat everything. After Ruth took the tray away, she helped
Emily up.

"Is there anything I can get you?" Ruth asked as soon as
Emily was settled in the rocking chair.

She looked down at the folds of the white gown that
enveloped her slender form. It must belong to Ruth. What
had that hateful man—that Adam Jacobs—done with her
things? "My bag," she said. "Is it here?"

"Yes." Ruth went to the corner of the room and brought
back the bag that contained all that remained of Emily's
earthly possessions. "I didn't want to rummage through

your things," she explained. "That's why you are wearing my gown." She smiled. "Though I must say, on you it looks more like a lace-embellished tent."

Ruth was a tall and large-framed young woman. Emily returned her smile. "I fear I'm a bit on the skinny side at the moment, but I'll fatten up in no time."

She opened her bag and removed a black Bible. "My papa gave this Bible to me on my twelfth birthday." She ran her hand gently over the worn leather cover.

"It looks as though you have made good use of it." Ruth sat down on the edge of the bed.

Emily lovingly caressed the book. "I have the past few months." She looked into Ruth's kind blue eyes. "When Jesus is all you have left, He becomes so much more precious to you."

"You know the Lord then?" Ruth leaned forward. "Have you been a believer long?"

"My, yes." Emily laughed then covered her mouth to stifle a cough before continuing. "Oh, please excuse me." She cleared her throat before continuing. "I can't remember when I didn't believe." Her face grew serious. "But I was twelve years old before I asked Jesus into my heart and gave my life to Him. I'd never have survived these times of trial without Him at my side."

"John and I lost our first baby two years ago," Ruth said. "We leaned heavily on the Lord to see us through that valley."

"I'm so sorry." Emily blinked back sympathetic tears. "Sometimes life can be very painful."

The two young women visited for several minutes until Emily began to grow weary. Ruth straightened the sheets and helped her into bed. She settled back against the pillows and clasped Ruth's hand. "Thank you for praying for me when I was so ill."

"You are welcome." Ruth squeezed her hand. "John and I both prayed for you."

"Yes, I know." Emily's eyes began to drift shut. "I heard your prayers."

five

On Friday afternoon, Ruth came into the bedroom where Emily sat in the rocking chair. She perched on the edge of the bed and smiled at the girl. "Do you feel strong enough to take a real bath?"

Emily looked up from the Bible that lay open on her lap. "Do you mean in a tub with soap and hot water?"

"I do." Ruth grinned. "Do you feel up to it?"

Emily's eyes lit up. "I can't imagine anything feeling more wonderful."

"All right then. I'll heat the water." Ruth paused in the doorway. "Maybe you would like to wear your own nightgown."

"I'm tired of playing the invalid." Emily laid the Bible on the bedside table. "I want to get dressed."

"That sounds wonderful. You choose the dress, and I'll press it while you bathe."

After Ruth left to heat the water, Emily went to the old-fashioned clothes press where Ruth had hung her meager wardrobe. There wasn't much to choose from. Two dark-colored skirts and waists that looked like what they were—hand-me-downs. Well-worn and ill-fitting when she received them, they were practically threadbare after six months of wear in the waist factory. She pushed them aside and ran her hand over the green wool dress. This dress was her final gift from Mama and Papa. She hadn't worn it since the night of the fire.

"I shouldn't wear it for everyday." She took the dress down. "But I'm going to dress up for supper tonight."

Steam rose from the tub Ruth set up in front of the kitchen range. Emily glanced uneasily at the kitchen door. She hadn't expected to bathe in such a public place.

"Don't worry about the men," Ruth said. "John and Adam are out checking on the cattle. They brought most of them in before the storm hit, but there are always a few stragglers. They won't be back until suppertime, but just to be sure—"

Ruth latched the door then turned her back. Emily unbuttoned the white flannel nightgown and let it pool about her feet. She tested the water with the toes of her left foot. Hot! She jerked back, then gritted her teeth, stepped in, and gingerly lowered herself into the hot water. While she soaked, Ruth pressed her dress.

"Ruth, how soon do you think I can go into town?"

"Probably the middle of next week if it doesn't storm again."

She wished it could be sooner but knew she would need those few days to regain sufficient strength to search for work.

She closed her eyes and leaned back in the tub. All the stress and uncertainty of the past six months left her. From what she had been able to learn on the train, Sanctuary was a thriving community. Surely she would find work there.

After her bath, she sat wrapped in a quilt while Ruth brushed her hair. "I think I must have had ten pounds of soot in my hair," she said.

"You have beautiful hair," Ruth said. "My mother has dark hair. When I was a little girl, I wanted to have dark hair like Mama. My three brothers are blond like Daddy, too."

"Isn't it interesting that we usually want what we don't have?" Emily smiled. "I wanted to be tall like Papa."

"Your father is a tall man?"

"He was tall in my eyes. When I was a little girl, I thought Papa was the biggest, strongest man in the world."

"My daddy is tall and strong." Ruth drew the brush through Emily's damp hair. "He's six-feet-four-inches tall."

"My, that is tall. Papa was five-feet-nine, but he was a giant in my eyes." Papa had been a giant, maybe not physically, but spiritually. In her mind's eye, Emily saw her slender father, and a feeling of desolation washed over her. She quickly put her sorrow away. Mama and Papa were no longer a part of this fallen world. They were citizens of heaven now. Someday she would be reunited with them. They wouldn't want her to grieve.

"Emily." Ruth's gentle voice brought her back to this time and place. "Is your father gone?"

"Papa and Mama passed away in April."

Ruth's hand stopped in midstroke. "I am so sorry."

"Thank you. It was a difficult time." Emily clutched the quilt closer. She felt Ruth's gaze on her wrists. The broken skin was almost healed, but the wounds had been raw a week ago. She knew Ruth was curious about the marks, but it wasn't something she felt as though she could share. At least not yet. She changed the subject to the matter utmost in her mind. "Tell me about Sanctuary."

Ruth pulled up a chair facing Emily. "What do you want to know?"

"Everything, but mostly what my chances are of finding employment."

"There are between four and five hundred people in town. We have the usual businesses." Ruth's voice was thoughtful. "Daddy and Mama have a mercantile, but my brothers help out, so they rarely hire outside help. There's a barbershop. A blacksmith. A dressmaker. And, of course, a bank. That might be a possibility. The Sloans own the newspaper. We have three boardinghouses that sometimes hire women to cook and clean during harvesttime, but they would be slow now."

Emily's spirits sank. It didn't sound very promising. "Is that all?"

"We have four churches and the school." Ruth sighed. "That is about it, I'm afraid. The school is the biggest employer in Sanctuary. They hire eight teachers. My brother, Matthew, graduated from college last spring and started a four-year high school. It's too bad you aren't a teacher. Matt told me Miss Perkins, the young woman who teaches third and fourth grade, is leaving at the end of the month to get married."

"Papa was a professor of history. It was always my dream to follow in his footsteps." Emily felt a crushing wave of disappointment sweep over her. "Circumstances prevented me from completing my degree."

"I know it's rather presumptuous of me to ask, but how old are you, Emily?"

"I will be twenty-two in March," Emily said.

"Twenty-two?" Ruth's eyes twinkled. "Lewis Thompson's wife, Kirsten, is sixteen. And Adam thought—we all thought—you were probably no older than Kirsten."

"I suppose I appear younger than I am because I'm small."

"Perhaps," Ruth agreed with a smile. "My mother is small, and people used to mistake us for sisters."

Ruth hid a yawn behind her hand. "Excuse me; I can't imagine why I'm so tired."

Emily knew why Ruth was tired. She had spent the last week taking care of her, in addition to all her other chores.

"Ruth, I'm going to get dressed, then I am going to help you with supper."

"You aren't strong enough yet." Ruth rose in protest. "Besides, you might ruin your dress."

"I'll put on my work clothes." Emily gathered the quilt around her. "I can wear the dress another time. Maybe Sunday."

The two women spent the rest of the afternoon preparing

a special meal. Emily even made a raisin pie.

❧

Adam stepped through the kitchen door and stopped dead in his tracks. A woman was setting the table. A young woman with black hair pulled up in a twisted roll on the back of her head. The realization of who she was hit him with all the force of a sledgehammer. The mail-order bride. He hung his coat and hat on the coat rack beside the door. Should he speak to her or not? What should he say?

She looked at him. Her eyes were green. Emerald green. Strange he hadn't noticed that before. They sure were an unusual color. But pretty. Real pretty.

"Good afternoon, Miss Foster."

"Good afternoon, Mr. Jacobs."

She didn't look overly friendly. He recalled his actions at the depot. No wonder she was cool.

"It's good to see you looking so well."

"Thank you. I think I'm about back to normal." She joined Ruth at the stove.

Adam went into the parlor, where John was reading a magazine. He sat down in a cushioned chair. Through the doorway, he caught glimpses of the women as they moved between the stove and the table. Miss Foster was taller than he had first thought.

John turned a page. "She's pretty, isn't she?"

Adam started at the unexpected question and turned to his brother. "She's all right, I suppose."

John grinned at him. Actually, it was more of an irritating smirk than anything else. "Ruth told me she wants to go into town as soon as possible and look for work."

"Yeah. Well, she probably won't find anything this time of year."

"I don't know." John thumbed through the magazine.

"Ruth has a notion she might take Miss Perkins's place when she goes back to Billings."

"Miss Perkins, the teacher." Adam scoffed. "I doubt if she's qualified."

"She told Ruth she dropped out of school two months short of receiving her teaching certificate." John slouched back in his chair. "That might make a difference back East, but in Sanctuary that makes her highly qualified."

"Well, if I were Miss Foster, I wouldn't count my chickens before they hatched."

"That's why Ruth doesn't want us to say anything to her about the possibility that she might be hired. She doesn't want her to be disappointed."

"Yeah. Well, I'm not going to say anything to her about it." How old was Miss Foster? The question had been gnawing at Adam, but he hated to ask John. Sure as anything, he'd misconstrue simple curiosity as some kind of romantic interest.

"She's almost twenty-two."

Adam looked at his brother in surprise. How could he have known what he was thinking? John was still wearing that infuriating grin with a knowing look added on for good measure. So she was twenty-two. Well educated. Pretty. "Who cares," he growled.

John was still chuckling when Ruth called them to supper.

&

Every time Emily looked up from her plate, Adam Jacobs was looking at her. He averted his gaze before she could read the expression in his dark eyes, but she didn't imagine it was friendly.

Ruth asked about the cows and what damage the storm had done. John answered most of her questions. Adam offered only an occasional comment. Emily spoke when spoken to but was too tired to contribute much to the conversation. By the time Ruth offered generous slices of the raisin pie, it was all she could do to keep her eyes open.

John complimented her on the pie. About halfway through his piece of pie, Adam looked across the table at her.

"I guess you'll be leaving soon."

He couldn't be half as anxious to get rid of her as she was to go. "I'll leave as soon as possible," she replied. "Ruth thought it would be the middle of next week."

"Yeah. Well, I'll be happy to take you into town."

Overjoyed, no doubt. "John and Ruth can take me."

"You're my responsibility. I'll take you."

This big man was beginning to irritate her. "I am not your responsibility, Mr. Jacobs. I hereby absolve you of any ill-conceived obligation you may feel for my well-being."

That really sounded intelligent, Emily. This big oaf is going to think you are simpleminded in addition to whatever else he thinks about you.

"You are certainly an independent young lady, aren't you?" There was a twinkle in his eyes that set Emily's teeth on edge. "I find that—"

Considering her present situation, he probably found her independent spirit amusing. Or worse. Before he could finish his sentence, Emily jumped up. "It's time to clear the table."

She removed the plate with the remains of the raisin pie from in front of him. "Hey! I'm not finished with that."

The pie slid half off the plate when she slapped it back down in front of him. "If you want it, eat it."

"I guess I'd better before it goes in the slop bucket." He didn't even try to conceal the grin on his face.

Emily's face flushed as she helped Ruth gather the dishes from the table. Even if he did laugh at her, what would Mama think of her rude behavior? Mama had raised her to treat people with kindness. She would have been horrified at Emily's lack of manners. Mama would have suggested she apologize even if Mr. Jacobs was a big lout and deserved—

Is that the proper spirit for a Christian woman to display, Emily?

Emily sighed. "Please excuse my rudeness, Mr. Jacobs."

Adam looked up at her. "Huh?"

Wasn't once enough? Must she bear the humiliation of repeating her apology? "Please forgive my rude behavior. It was uncalled for."

"Oh, well." He wore a puzzled frown. "Sure, that's all right."

Out of the corner of her eye, she saw him exchange glances with John and shrug. He had no idea why she was apologizing. The whole humiliating experience had been unnecessary. She managed not to look at him as she carried the stack of dishes to the sink. The men finished their pie and went into the parlor while the two women washed dishes and put the kitchen in order.

"Are you too tired to join us in the parlor?" Ruth asked when the last pan had been dried and put away.

Her anger at Adam Jacobs had subsided, leaving her feeling drained. "Maybe some other night, Ruth. Right now all I want to do is sleep."

"I understand. You have put in quite a day after having been so ill." Ruth hugged the younger woman. "You go on to bed. I'll see you in the morning."

After she was in her nightgown, Emily opened the door to let heat in from the kitchen. She fell asleep before she completed her prayers that night.

૨૦

It was early morning before she stirred. Faint lamplight drifted through the open door of the bedroom. *Ruth must already be up and preparing breakfast.* She started to throw the covers back, then she heard the murmur of Ruth's and John's voices coming from the kitchen, and she realized they were talking about her.

"It's hard telling what she's been through since her parents died," Ruth said. "She doesn't talk about her past, but I know from what she said yesterday, she was raised in a loving, Christian home."

"Both parents died at the same time?" John paused. Emily imagined him sipping the hot coffee she could smell. "They must have been killed in an accident."

"Has Adam said anything about her? I mean—" Ruth's next words were indistinct. *She must be standing at the cabinet rolling out biscuits.*

Emily heard a chair being pushed back and figured John was refilling his coffee cup. He said something she couldn't make out. Then she heard his chair creaking as he sat back down. "It's time Adam moved on with his life. He's moped long enough."

"I know, but it's difficult for him. First your dad, then—" She opened the oven door and slid the pan of biscuits in, muffling whatever she said next.

"Gertrude Phillips wasn't worth grieving over." John snorted.

"That may be," Ruth agreed. "But Adam—" The sizzling of frying bacon being turned masked Ruth's next words.

"Adam told me—" John replied, but Emily couldn't make out the rest of his words. She slipped close to the door where she could hear better. "That is probably true," Ruth said. "But Adam has been in a spirit of rebellion for several years. I think Gertrude may have been part of that rebellion, John."

"No doubt she was," John answered. "If not for his anger, Adam would never have given her a second look."

"Adam seems to think God has singled him out for punishment."

"Well, it's time he got over that." Emily heard the concern in John's voice. "Until he makes things right with the Lord, he'll never find peace."

"I think Emily may be just what Adam needs."

"You are a born matchmaker, honey." John chuckled softly. "But I think you'd better give up on this one."

"Maybe God sent Emily to help Adam."

They stopped talking, and Emily slipped back to her bed and snuggled down under the covers to consider what she had overheard. Adam Jacobs had been in love with a woman named Gertrude, who abandoned him.

No wonder; as hateful as he is, it's unlikely any woman could put up with him for long.

That was an uncharitable thought, Emily.

"I know," Emily whispered in reply to the small, ever-present voice of her conscience. "I'm sorry."

Adam Jacobs is a Christian brother who is out of fellowship with the Lord.

Emily was quick to defend herself, her words slipping from whisper to thought. *Yes, but that's not my fault.*

She remembered her first meeting with Adam and frowned. *He talked about me as though I had no more feelings than the bench I was sitting on.*

You have always been safe in the arms of the Shepherd, Emily. Adam Jacobs is outside the fold.

But that's his own fault. He chose to be angry.

The Shepherd grieves when His sheep stray.

I know. She had been having conversations with her inner voice since she was a little girl. She had learned long ago that it was useless to argue. The still, small voice was always right. But what could she do?

Pray for the sheep that has strayed, Emily.

But I don't like him. Emily knew it was her final argument.

It sounded whiny even to her. *He's. . .he's. . .*

The Shepherd knows what he is, Emily. You must pray for him.

I will. Emily sighed. *But I still don't like him. I don't hate him, of course. I just don't. . .* She stopped to think of the correct word. *He's infuriating.*

It doesn't matter. The Shepherd loves him, just as He loves you. Pray, Emily.

Her whispered prayer was short and reflected more duty than emotion, but under the circumstances, she felt it was the best she could do.

Emily sat back up on the side of the bed. Before she could stand, she heard the back door open.

"It's colder than the North Pole out there." The outside door closed, but not before a gust of frigid air swept across the room and nipped at her bare feet.

"That man is such an aggravation," she grumbled to herself as she ran across the icy floor to the bedroom door. She caught a glimpse of Mr. Jacobs standing in front of Ruth's stove warming his backside before she slammed the door with a resounding thump.

૪

"I see your houseguest is in a good mood this morning." Adam grinned.

"I think you hurt her feelings last night at supper." Ruth nudged him aside to remove the biscuits from the oven.

"Me? What did I do? I offered to take her to town. I ate a piece of her pie. By the way, do you think I could have another piece for breakfast? No offense to you, Ruth, but that was about the best raisin pie I've ever eaten."

"Why didn't you tell her so?" Ruth put her hands on her hips. "Forevermore, Adam, pour yourself a cup of coffee and get out of my way."

"Well, I might have told her if she'd given me a chance." Adam filled his mug and sat down at the table. "She practically ripped the fork out of my hand."

The bedroom door opened, and the mail-order bride walked into the room with her head held high. "Good morning, Ruth. John." She took one of Ruth's aprons from a hook on the wall and tied it around her waist.

So she didn't intend to speak to him. Well, he'd just see about that. "Good morning, Miss Foster."

"Good morning, Mr. Jacobs." She offered him a disdainful glance before turning to Ruth. "What can I do to help?"

Ruth stood at the sink, straining the morning's milking he'd just brought in from the barn. "Would you like to make gravy?"

"Of course." Adam watched as Emily sifted flour and stirred it into the hot bacon grease in the skillet. She continued to stir as Ruth poured milk from a pitcher into the mixture. "I think it's just right," she said.

After Emily sprinkled pepper and salt in, she poured the thickened gravy into an earthenware bowl and set it in the middle of the table. Adam thought he could pull her chair out and see that she was seated, but before he had a chance to stand, she slipped gracefully into the chair across the table from him. After John offered thanks for the food, they ate; then Adam walked with his brother out to the barn.

six

"You have a piano." Emily stood in the parlor doorway. "Do you play?"

"I wish I could," Ruth said. "But the piano belonged to John's mother."

Crossing the room to stand in front of the gleaming instrument, Emily gently caressed the closed cover of the keyboard.

"Do you play?" Ruth asked.

"I've played since I was three years old." Emily touched the hymnal on the music stand.

"Would you play something for me?" Ruth perched on the edge of the couch.

"Oh, I don't know." Emily's fingers tingled with her desire to touch the keys. "It's been almost seven months since I've been near a piano. I probably should practice first."

"Practice for me," Ruth urged. "Then tonight you can play for John and Adam."

"Promise not to expect too much." Emily sat down on the piano bench and thumbed through the hymnal. Having made her selection, she uncovered the keyboard and began to play.

The music flowed from her fingertips as she played hymn after hymn. Her fingers fell silent on the keyboard as the clock on the mantel chimed nine times.

"Oh, Ruth, I'm so sorry." She closed the hymnal. "You should have stopped me."

Ruth moved to the bench beside Emily. "Why would I stop you? Listening to you, I caught a glimpse of heaven. Who taught you to play like that?"

"Mama." Emily slowly lowered the cover over the keyboard. "She taught music before she married Papa." She brushed at the corner of her eye. "I guess we'd better get the cleaning done before it's time to go back to the kitchen."

"Will you play for us tonight?" Ruth asked as the two young women set about cleaning the parlor.

"Perhaps." Emily's smile didn't quite make it to her eyes.

"Are you all right?"

"I am," Emily said. "It's just that sometimes I miss Mama and Papa so much, I can hardly bear it."

"I'm so sorry." Ruth reached out to the younger woman.

Emily grasped her hand. "It's all right, Ruth. I know that someday I will see them again. They wouldn't want me to grieve."

❧

After breakfast, Adam and John rode across the snow-covered pastures looking for five head of cattle that were still unaccounted for. A mile from the house, they found the remains of a yearling steer.

"Looks like wolves got him," John observed as he knelt beside the half-eaten carcass.

"Yeah, I guess so." Adam fought against the sick feeling that gripped his stomach. "We should have gotten them in sooner."

"There's nothing can be done about it now." John stood and swung back into the saddle.

"Yeah. Well, if I hadn't had to make that trip into town, we could have gotten them all in."

The brothers rode across the white landscape in silence for several minutes. "This is all Lewis Thompson's fault," Adam said. "If he hadn't stuck his big nose into my business, I would have had time to help round up the cattle before the storm hit."

"How long you planning to be mad at Lewis?"

"Why shouldn't I be mad at him?" Adam scowled. "Because of him, we've lost five head of cattle, and I'm saddled with that woman. You know how hard it's going to be getting her settled in Sanctuary?"

"I thought you liked Emily."

"I guess you thought wrong," Adam growled and slumped in the saddle.

John didn't say anything more for some time until two riders topped the horizon. "Isn't that Ike and Lewis?"

Adam saw the two approaching horsemen. "Yeah, that's the Thompson brothers." He'd recognize the two lanky, loose-jointed men anywhere. Nobody sat a saddle quite like Lewis. "They're trespassing."

"Lewis and Ike have been our friends since we were boys, Adam. They are not trespassing."

"Lewis Thompson is no friend of mine. A friend wouldn't do what Lewis has done to me."

"Hey, Ike!" John raised a hand in greeting. "Hey, Lewis!"

John reined his horse in, and Adam had no choice but to bring Copper to a reluctant standstill. The brothers rode up alongside them. "Hey, John! Adam. Glad we run into you," Ike said. "We got four of your heifers over at our place."

"Great," John said with a smile. "We found a dead steer back a ways, and we figured the other four were dead, too."

"We just rounded them up with ours."

Adam sat apart from John and the brothers while Ike and John made small talk. Lewis nudged his horse over to Adam. "How's things going, Adam?"

"How do you think things are going?" Adam glared at his former best friend.

"Look, Adam, I'm real sorry about what I done." Lewis bunched the reins between his big hands.

A gust of wintry wind tugged at Adam's muffler. He hardened his heart against any warm feelings he might have for the other man. "You got me into a real mess, Lewis Thompson."

Lewis looked down. His windburned face twisted in misery. "I didn't mean to, Adam. I just wanted you to be happy again."

Adam glared at Lewis before turning his head and looking toward the snow-covered mountains.

"Did you send her back?"

The anger that lurked in a dark corner of Adam's heart lashed out. "No, I did not send her back." He swung around to face Lewis. "She was so sick when she got off the train, I thought she was going to die before I got her to Ruth. As soon as the storm let up, I rode into Sanctuary and brought Doc Brown out to see about her. It took me half a day to make a one-hour trip. I didn't need this kind of trouble, Lewis. My life was going along just fine before you butted into it."

"Is she all right?"

"She's fine. As soon as the weather clears and I can get her into town, I'm going to find a place to leave her." Adam huffed. "You ought to be the one doing that. She should be your responsibility, Lewis Thompson. Not mine."

"I'm sorry, Adam. I know I already said that, but I wish you'd believe me."

Lewis looked near tears, but Adam refused to be moved by his obvious pain. Considering what he'd done to him, Adam figured Lewis deserved to suffer. "We've been friends almost as long as I can remember, Adam. You and me, we've had some adventures together. And, well, ever since your dad died, you've been different."

Adam wanted to deny what Lewis said, but he couldn't. Starting with the death of his dad, he'd watched his world crumble around him. Anyone who was forced to stand by helplessly and watch his dreams stomped into the dust would be angry.

"Yeah, well maybe I am different." He lashed out at Lewis. "If I am, I've got reason to be. God had no call to make me His whipping boy."

Lewis swallowed a couple of times as his hands curled into fists. "You know, Adam, it's one thing to be mad at me—maybe you should be—but you've got no right to be mad at God. I'm sorry for what I done, and I hope someday you can find it in your heart to forgive me. But until you get down on your knees and square things with God, you're going to keep right on being miserable."

Adam pulled Copper around and urged his ride away through the drifting snow, leaving Lewis behind.

John caught up and rode alongside him for a while in silence. "Ike said we could leave those heifers at their place long as we want."

Adam hunkered down and didn't say anything. John glanced at his younger brother. "Guess you and Lewis didn't settle your differences."

"You know what he had the nerve to tell me? He said until I made things right with God, I would never be happy."

When John didn't respond, Adam turned away to ride home in silence. They were approaching the barn before John replied, "Lewis is right, Adam."

Adam turned to look at his brother. "About what?"

"About you being out of fellowship with the Lord."

"God abandoned me, John."

John swung down from his horse and opened the barn door. They unsaddled the horses and curried them in silence.

After Copper and John's horse, Midnight, were in their stalls and hay had been thrown down to the cows, John asked, "You want to milk or gather eggs?"

"I'll milk." Adam took the bucket and a one-legged stool and went into the stall with the cow. While she chewed contentedly on a manger full of hay, he put the pail between his feet, rested his head against her warm flank, and milked. The white milk foamed into the bucket until it was almost full. After he had stripped the last drop from her, he hung the stool on the wall.

John had several eggs in a straw-lined basket. "You can take the milk to the house with you." Adam handed his brother the bucket.

"Aren't you coming in?"

"I thought I'd clean up a bit before I come over." He ran his hand over his bearded face. "Maybe shave."

John grinned but didn't say anything. He paused at the door. "You know, Adam, that mountain you see in the distance has probably been there at least since the Genesis flood. Wouldn't you say?"

"Yeah, I guess so." Adam frowned.

"Thousands of years, right?"

Adam nodded. "Ever since the floodwaters receded at least."

"Hasn't ever moved, has it?"

Adam snorted. "Of course not."

"If you walked long enough, kept your eye on the mountain, and stayed the course, you could walk right up to it. Isn't that right?"

"You know you could," Adam said. What was John getting at?

"If you walked away, and you walked far enough, I suppose you would reach a point where you couldn't see the mountain anymore."

Adam shuffled his feet. Why didn't John say what he wanted to say before they both got frostbite?

"If you traveled so far away you couldn't see the mountain, would that be because the mountain wasn't there anymore?"

"Look, John, it's cold out here and this is the last ridiculous question I'm going to answer. The mountain doesn't move. If I travel far enough away so that I can't see it, it's because I'm the one who has moved. Now I'm going to my house and get cleaned up. See you later."

He started to walk away when John called his name. He turned back. "What?"

"God doesn't move, either, little brother."

So even John was down on him. Adam stewed all the way to his house. It wasn't his fault Dad died and he had to quit school. Then God took Mom, right when Adam needed her the most. Then Gertrude—well, it didn't really matter about Trudy. Her leaving was a relief. At least it was until everyone started feeling sorry for him. But Lewis sending for that mail-order bride—well, that was the last straw.

He went into his cabin, letting the door slam behind him, and stepped on an open magazine. Books, magazines, and newspapers lay where they had been dropped from one end of the cabin to the other. Various articles of clothing formed a heap on the floor by his bed. A shirt hung from the back of a chair at the table. An inch of dust covered the few pieces of furniture, and the floor hadn't been swept for months. The bedcovers lay in a twisted heap in the middle of the unmade bed. Cobwebs swayed in the corners.

"No self-respecting hog would live in this mess," Adam muttered.

After putting a kettle of water on the box heater, he wrestled the bedclothes into some semblance of order, then sat down on the bed. With the toe of his boot, he pushed a pile of magazines into an untidy heap, then shoved them under the bed with his heel. It would take him days—maybe even weeks—to get this place in order. How did Ruth manage? Her house was always neat as a pin. So was Bertha Thompson's, and she had a baby to take care of.

Of course, not all women were so tidy. When Lewis's child bride had her own house, he bet it wouldn't be much cleaner than his cabin. Serve Lewis right if he had to live the rest of his days in squalor. He stood and stretched. What else could a man expect? Buying a wife out of a magazine.

He stripped off his shirt and set about making himself presentable. Freshly scrubbed and shaved, he rummaged around until he found a clean shirt that wasn't too wrinkled. Forty-five minutes later, Adam walked into his brother's kitchen.

&

Emily glanced up when the back door opened, then looked quickly away. My, oh my! What a difference a shave and a bit of soap and water made. Adam Jacobs was a handsome man. She stole a glance at the man talking to John. Who would ever have imagined such a face was hiding under that horrible beard? He looked up, and their eyes met. Emily's heart lurched. She lowered her gaze and finished setting the table.

After supper, the two men went into the parlor, leaving the women alone with the dishes. Ruth slipped the heavy cast-iron skillet into the oven and hung up the dish towel. "You will join us in the parlor tonight, won't you?"

"Well, I. . ." She really should refuse. "I think I would enjoy that."

"Good!" Ruth hung her apron on a hook beside the stove. "You can play for us."

Both men were reading when Ruth and Emily came into the parlor.

"I discovered something wonderful today," Ruth announced without preamble. "Emily plays the piano. And, I might add, she plays magnificently." She gave Emily a little nudge. "Play for us, Emily."

Emily hesitated until John smiled at her. "We would enjoy listening to you, Miss Foster. We haven't had much music in this house since Mom left us."

"If you're sure it wouldn't disturb you."

"We'd enjoy a musical evening, wouldn't we, Adam?"

"Sure, go ahead, Miss Foster."

Emily slid onto the piano bench and began to play. After the first song, Ruth joined her on the bench and sang while Emily played. She would have loved to join in on the singing but feared she'd fall into a coughing jag if she did. John soon pulled out his fiddle. Finally, Adam opened a case that was leaning on the wall beside the piano and brought out his guitar.

The others sang several hymns as Emily played, then she struck up a lively rendition of "Yankee Doodle" followed by "Camptown Races."

They were all laughing when she closed the piano. "I think that is enough for tonight," she said.

"I hope we haven't worn you out," Ruth said.

"Not at all." Emily smiled. "I can't recall when I've enjoyed an evening more."

"This house has been too long without music and laughter." John returned his fiddle to its velvet-lined case. "Isn't that so, Adam?"

Adam shrugged as he returned his guitar to its place beside the piano. "I'll check the cattle before I go to my cabin." As he left the room, he muttered, "See you in the morning."

In the privacy of her small room, Emily pulled her flannel nightgown over her head and undressed in its tented warmth before sticking her arms through the sleeves. With the full moon reflecting off the snow, it was light as midafternoon outside. She took her Bible and moved to the lone window. The pages fell open to the photograph concealed inside. The green dress, the photograph, and her Bible were the only things remaining from her past. She held the photograph to the light and studied their dear faces. Papa with his neatly trimmed beard. Mama with her wide green eyes, so like Emily's own, except Mama's eyes were sightless.

Mama "saw" through the delicate touch of her fingers. Emily was six years old before she realized that her mother couldn't actually see through her fingertips, as Emily had always believed. Mama had never seen her face or Papa's face. Mama had never seen a sunrise. Or a sunset. Or the beautiful flowers. When she wept at the sadness of it, Mama's arms had comforted her.

"Oh, Emily, darling." Mama laughed softly. "Never weep for me. I have a wonderful life. And someday, when the Father calls me home, I will be able to see. Just think, Emily, the very first thing I shall ever see will be my Master's face. Then, Emily, after that, all the glory of heaven awaits me. Can you imagine? Oh, Emily, can you even begin to imagine how wonderful that will be?"

"Now all the glory of heaven is yours, Mama." Emily brushed a tear from her eye. "How happy you and Papa must be."

She replaced the photograph, and a verse caught her attention. "Rejoice in the Lord alway: and again I say, Rejoice."

She read the remainder of the fourth chapter of Philippians. The eleventh verse had been one of her mother's favorites, and she often quoted it.

" 'Not that I speak in respect of want,' " Emily read the familiar words aloud. " 'For I have learned, in whatsoever state I am, therewith to be content.' "

How precious those words were. Emily finished the chapter,

then closed her Bible and laid it on the bedside table. She shivered in the cold, then scooted across the floor to open the door and let in heat. Diving into bed, she pulled the mountain of quilts over her.

Curled under the covers, she whispered the nineteenth verse. " 'But my God shall supply all your need according to His riches in glory by Christ Jesus.' "

Snuggling deeper into her nest, she began to pray. "Dear Lord, Sanctuary isn't very large. I know it is going to take a miracle for me to find work. But You are the God of impossible situations. You saved me from those horrible men and brought me here. There is no task too large for You. In Thee I place my trust."

Wrapped in the cocoon of slowly warming quilts, she thought of the evening just past. Adam—Mr. Jacobs—certainly had musical talent. His long fingers fairly danced over the strings of his guitar. Her thoughts turned to Gertrude—the woman she had overheard John and Ruth talking about earlier—the woman Adam Jacobs had loved.

He still loves her. A sharp pain stabbed through her chest. *Now what was that about, Emily? You don't even like Adam Jacobs. Why should you care if he is in love with this woman? This Gertrude.*

Emily managed to roll to her side beneath the weight of the quilts. Adam had obviously been hurt deeply by something in his past. Probably that woman, Gertrude. Surely, it wasn't God's will for him to carry a hurt such as this for so long. She remembered Ruth's words. *Adam is in a spirit of rebellion.*

She recalled her father saying, "There is no man more miserable than the believer out of fellowship with his Creator."

Tears filled Emily's eyes and overflowed. Adam Jacobs was living proof of the truth of her father's words. Her heart ached for him. Always before, she had prayed for him out of a sense of duty. Tonight her prayer was a heartfelt, impassioned plea for Adam Jacobs to find his way home.

seven

The sun shone brightly all day Thursday. The snow began to melt and slide off the houses and barns. Saturday, the men did chores in their shirtsleeves. By midmorning on Tuesday, the roads were dry enough to be passable. John hitched up the wagon and took Emily and Ruth to town.

As soon as they entered Reed's General Store, a small, dark-haired woman rushed around the counter to embrace Ruth. "That was some storm, wasn't it? We had to close the store for three days. How were things at the ranch? Where is John?"

"He went to the barbershop. We hibernated during the blizzard." Ruth laid her hand on Emily's arm. "Mom, I want you to meet my friend, Miss Emily Foster. Emily, this is my mother, Mrs. Margaret Reed. Emily has been spending some time with us."

"I'm pleased to meet you." Emily smiled her gratitude that Ruth had not introduced her as Adam's mail-order bride. Rejected mail-order bride. Although she had no doubt the circumstances of her arrival would travel quickly in this small town, she preferred to pretend people weren't whispering about her behind their hands.

After a few moments of small talk with Mrs. Reed, Ruth asked, "Where is Daddy? I want Emily to meet him."

"He's in the storeroom. You girls go on back and visit with him while I wait on my customers."

Ruth had told her the general store stocked everything from shovels to crackers to dress goods. Still, she wasn't prepared for the seemingly endless variety of items that overflowed the shelves, hung from the exposed rafters of the high ceiling, and filled every available corner of the large store. She looked around wide-eyed as she followed Ruth through the clutter.

"Believe me," Ruth said over her shoulder, "there is a method to this. Mom and Daddy and the boys know where every single thing in this store is located. I did, too, until I married John. Now I doubt I could find anything."

She pushed open one of a pair of wide swinging doors, and Emily followed her into a room piled high with boxes, crates, and barrels. "Daddy, are you here?"

"Is that my princess?" A huge blond man stepped from behind a stack of boxes and caught Ruth up in a giant bear hug that lifted her off her feet. Then he gently lowered her until her feet touched the floor. "Mama says I'm going to have to be less exuberant in my greeting for a few months now." His broad face beamed. "I was mighty happy to hear your news, Ruthie."

Ruth patted her father's arm and blushed becomingly. Ruth was expecting! Emily turned startled eyes toward her new friend. Why hadn't she realized Ruth's condition?

You have been too caught up in your own problems to take notice of anyone else, her small inner voice whispered. She didn't bother to argue. Her conscience smote her when she thought of the extra work she had caused Ruth.

"Daddy, this is our houseguest, Emily Foster." Ruth drew Emily forward. "She came to us in the blizzard."

The man's huge hand enveloped hers. "Ah, yes! Miss Foster, welcome to Sanctuary."

"I'm pleased to meet you, Mr. Reed." Emily slipped her hand from his. "Ruth has told me so much about you."

"Has she now?" The man's smile was open and friendly. "That puts you at an advantage, Emily. I know very little about you."

Very little, perhaps, but he had heard of her. She could tell by his expression that he knew why she was in Sanctuary. The young man at the railroad station probably announced the circumstances of her arrival to everyone in town. This was a good place to begin to squelch the rumors that must be circulating about her.

She looked up, up, up into Mr. Reed's gentle blue eyes. "I did not come here with the intention of marrying Adam Jacobs. It was always my father's dream to come west. A dream I came to share. When the opportunity presented itself in a most unexpected—and one might say miraculous—way, I accepted it as an answer to prayer. I plan to make Sanctuary my home. In order to do that, I need to find employment as soon as possible. I am not proud. I will accept anything that is honorable."

Ruth spoke then. "Emily is looking for work, Daddy. Do you know of any positions in town?"

Emily took a deep breath as her carefully maintained reserve began to crumple. "Please, sir, I would appreciate any help you can give me."

"Well, now." He rubbed his bearded chin. "Let's sit down, put our heads together, and see what we can come up with." He pulled off his white apron and spread it over a large crate. "Have a seat, girls."

Emily perched on the crate beside Ruth, and he sat on a barrel facing them. "Now, Emily, what experience have you had?"

"For the past several months, I worked in a shirtwaist factory."

"I'm afraid there isn't any call for that type of work in Sanctuary."

His voice was gentle and his tone so kind and concerned, Emily felt her lower lip begin to tremble. "No, I knew there were no factories."

"Is there anything else you might have an aptitude for?"

"Mama became ill a few months before I graduated from college, and I wasn't able to complete my education. I had hoped to teach school like my father did." She looked down at her hands, then into the kind eyes of Ruth's father. "I took care of Mama until her death."

The compassion in his expression gave her courage to continue. "There was a fire last April, and Mama and Papa went home to be with the Lord."

Ruth squeezed Emily's clasped hands. "I didn't know. I'm so sorry, Emily."

"Thank you, Ruth, but it's all right. Mama and Papa are in heaven now. They wouldn't want me to grieve for them."

"Still, you were left all alone."

"I am alone." She pulled her hands from Ruth's gentle grasp. "That is why I must secure employment as soon as possible. Can you help me, Mr. Reed?"

"Perhaps I can." Mr. Reed scratched at his beard. "Let me talk to a few people."

"Thank you, sir." Emily rose and extended her hand.

The big man clasped her hand in his. "As soon as I know something for certain, I'll let you know. It should be by the end of this week." He answered her unasked question.

The built-up tension left Emily's body. "Thank you, Mr. Reed. Thank you so much."

The two young women returned to the front of the store to find John leaning against the counter talking to his mother-in-law. While Ruth and John did their shopping, Emily browsed and chatted with Mrs. Reed between customers.

That evening, when Ruth and Emily joined the men in the parlor, John was immersed in the newspaper he had bought in town. Adam sat on the couch strumming idly on his guitar. Ruth sat down and took up her knitting.

Each evening, Emily had watched Ruth's needles flash

in and out, but until this evening, she hadn't paid attention to what she was knitting. She thought back over the last six months and realized she had pulled her emotions inward. How long had it been since she had reached out to anyone? From the moment of her parents' deaths, she had thought only of her own pain. Her own survival. Remorse filled her heart.

She sat down at the piano with her back to the others and began to play softly while silent tears coursed down her cheeks. Peace filled her heart as she continued to play.

She began to hum softly as her fingers found the melody of a song of praise. After a few choruses, Adam moved to stand beside the piano. He positioned his guitar and began to play.

As their music blended, Emily joined in singing. "Praise the Lord, praise the Lord, let the earth hear His voice." Her voice still tender from her recent illness, she sang softly and let the words cleanse her soul. "Praise the Lord, praise the Lord, let the people rejoice."

When she reached the end of the song, she glanced up at Adam and smiled. Then she turned to watch Ruth's knitting needles form the tiny sweater. "When is the child coming?"

Ruth's cheeks grew rosy as she looked up. "In April, God willing."

"Oh, Ruth, I know how concerned you must be, but surely God will give you this child." Emily spoke from a heart overflowing with love and concern. "I will pray for you and your new little one."

"Thank you, Emily. I welcome your prayers." Her hands grew still as her gaze met Emily's. "I would like to ask you something if you don't mind."

Emily smiled. "I guess I won't know if I mind until after you ask."

Ruth returned her smile. "No, I guess you won't."

Her expression grew serious. "Today, when you told Daddy about losing your parents, I thought how courageous you were. How were you able to endure such a tremendous loss?"

John didn't look up from his newspaper. Adam continued to strum his guitar from the chair to which he had returned. Although neither of the brothers seemed to be listening, Emily could sense a tenseness in the room as they waited for her reply. She looked slowly from one member of the Jacobs family to the other. These three people had taken her in and cared for her when she had nowhere else to go. Her eyes rested for a moment on Adam, his head bent over the guitar. Even he, despite his surliness at their first meeting, had shown compassion for her. Bringing her to Ruth, when he could just as well have left her in the train station to fend for herself. And then, when she couldn't get well on her own, he had ridden through the storm to bring a doctor.

Her gaze moved to John before coming to rest once more on Ruth. Their prayers had penetrated the cloud of darkness that surrounded her as they petitioned God for her healing. She owed her life to John and Ruth and Adam.

"It hasn't been easy, Ruth. At first I questioned God." Emily gripped the edge of the piano bench and lowered her head. "I was even angry at Him for a while."

"That's understandable." Ruth looked at the tiny garment in her hands. "I'm sure most of us feel that way when we experience a great loss."

"But it was wrong of me. In my anger and confusion, I made some very foolish decisions." Emily lifted her head and looked directly into Adam's dark eyes. "I couldn't endure the platitudes and words of comfort. What did these people— my church family—know of my pain? One night I left everything that was familiar, and taking what little money I had, I moved into a most undesirable neighborhood. A week later,

I went to work at the Triangle Shirtwaist Company."

She pleated her skirt between her fingers. "Mama and Papa always taught me that Jesus would never leave me. But to my shame, for a brief period, I left Him. This was the loneliest, most miserable time of my life. After a week at the shirtwaist factory, I started attending church services at an inner-city mission. The ministers seemed to be different every Sunday, and the congregation was composed mainly of transients. I never made friends there, but I reconnected with my dearest and most faithful Friend. Without my Savior, I would never have survived the next few months."

Emily fell silent, and Ruth asked, "That is why you became a mail-order bride? To escape the city?"

"Yes. But it didn't happen the way you may have imagined." A gentle smile lifted the corners of Emily's mouth. "The Triangle Shirtwaist Company was a terrible place. The girls who worked there were little more than slaves. The International Ladies Garment Workers Union was trying to organize the workers so conditions might be improved. There was stiff opposition from the factory owners. Several of the girls disappeared. Gossip had it they were killed because of their support of the union."

Her gaze came to rest on Ruth. "I don't know if this was true or not because of what happened to me, but at the time I believed it. However, I was an outspoken supporter of the union. So outspoken that I lost my job." She laughed softly. "It's amazing how God took what I considered a great tragedy and used it to display His love for me. I was walking home that evening, wondering how I would survive the coming winter and praying, when I was abducted by two men."

"Oh, Emily!" Ruth gasped. "I had no idea."

"What they meant for evil, God used for good. I was blindfolded and bound hand and foot." She rubbed her wrist.

"I know you must have wondered about these marks."

"Yes, we have."

"I struggled to escape, but of course it was impossible." Her shoulders rose and fell. "They took me to a ramshackle old building and locked me in a room. That night I decided, even if they killed me, I would do nothing to dishonor God. The following morning, I learned the girls imprisoned in this house would be auctioned off to"—the color rose in her face—"to bad places."

She noticed John had put his newspaper to one side, and Adam's fingers rested on the strings of a silent guitar. "They took us downstairs where the buyers were waiting. Among them was a man who offered me the opportunity to come west."

Her gaze came to rest on Adam. "I had no intention of marrying you, Mr. Jacobs. But when Mr. Smith told me I would have six months to make a decision, I signed the contract. As soon as I secure employment, I will repay the money I owe the Thompson brothers."

After a brief silence, Ruth spoke. "Today, when you told Daddy about losing your parents, I thought how brave you were. Now I realize you are even more courageous than I first thought."

"I'm not as courageous as you think, Ruth. I have plunged into the depths of despair. I have questioned God many times. Papa was a professor of history. I always wanted to follow in his footsteps. To teach. When Mama became ill, I abandoned my dreams. Much as I loved her, it was very difficult for me to accept that I was never going to be a teacher."

"You came so close," Ruth soothed. "It's understandable that you would resent the loss of your dream."

"My dream, Ruth. Mine. Not God's. Don't you see?" Emily lifted her hand toward Ruth, then let it drop back in her lap.

"What God had planned for me was much more wonderful than anything I could have imagined."

"Why would you say that?" Adam leaned forward. "You lost everything."

"I wouldn't exchange a dozen college degrees for the years I spent caring for Mama." Tears filled her eyes. "Mama lost her sight when she was two years old. But she never lost her vision of heaven. Mama loved the Word, and we memorized many verses together. Recently I have found great comfort in one of them. Isaiah 43:2 strengthens me."

Emily rose from the piano bench. "I shall retire now if you have no objections."

"No, you've had a busy day." Ruth rolled up her knitting and put it to one side. "We'll see you in the morning."

"Good night." She paused at the door and turned. "Thank you for all you have done for me." A smile lit up her face. "Isn't God wonderful?"

Then she was gone.

eight

That night, lying on his bed in the cabin, sleep eluded Adam. Every time he closed his eyes, he saw Emily Foster's face. In the beginning, when he first met her, he thought she was a rather unremarkable-looking young woman. Not homely. But certainly not beautiful. Tonight, watching her sing, then later listening to the things she said, he thought he had never seen anyone lovelier. Emily's acceptance of her parents' deaths and her assurance that Jesus walked beside her brought Adam under a conviction far deeper than the one that had led to his conversion at the age of fifteen.

"When thou passest through the waters, I will be with thee; and through the rivers, they shall not overflow thee: when thou walkest through the fire, thou shalt not be burned; neither shall the flame kindle upon thee."

Isaiah 43:2. The verse Emily had mentioned. He looked it up in his Bible before he went to bed. The words ran through his mind. *I will be with thee. I will be. . .with thee. I. . .God. . . will be with. . .thee. . .Adam. I will be with you through the floods and the fires. God walks beside me through the good times and the bad. When did I quit believing that? When did I turn away from God?*

Six years ago, he had been a freshman at college in Billings. Then his father was killed in a senseless accident. He left school and returned home. His dream of being a doctor was buried with his father. By the time his mom died four years later, Ruth and John were married. He built the one-room cabin.

Then Gertrude came into his life. Beautiful, flirtatious

Trudy Phillips. That first Sunday at church, they shared a hymnal, and he fell head over heels in love with her. Two weeks later, they were engaged. Talk about foolish decisions!

A derisive laugh burst from his lips. Fortunately, she ran away before he could compound his stupidity by marrying her.

When had it started? His pulling away from God. Was it when his dad was killed? When he was forced to give up his dream? When his mother died?

He threw his arm across his eyes. It didn't really matter when it began. The past six years had been miserable. He cried out in the still of the night, "Oh, Father, forgive me!"

Tossing the tangled covers aside, he dropped to his knees beside the bed and cried out to the Lord until the sheet was wet with his tears. As the forgiving grace of his heavenly Father washed over him, a joy he had almost forgotten flooded his soul.

Finally, he got to his feet, straightened the covers, and crawled back into bed. For the first time in months, he fell into a peaceful, refreshing sleep.

He woke at daybreak the next morning. After building up the fire, he dressed, pulled on his boots, grabbed his coat and hat, and went outside. The sky was a glory of crimson and gold as the sun peeked over the eastern horizon. The mountains were still a shadowy mass to the west. How long had it been since he noticed the glory of God's creation? Like a blind man whose sight had been restored, he stretched his arms wide, threw back his head, and shouted to the heavens, "Thank You, Lord!"

"It is awe-inspiring, isn't it?"

Adam turned quickly. Emily stood behind him, her ragged old coat pulled tightly around her. "I have dreamed about the West ever since I can remember. I never imagined the vastness. Or the splendor."

It was awe-inspiring! Adam laughed aloud with the wonder. He rose before dawn every morning, but for the last six years, he had been too bitter to see the wonder of what lay around him. "I don't remember the last time I noticed the sunrise. It is magnificent, isn't it?"

"Yes, it is." Emily's smile rivaled the sun. "Truly magnificent."

She was beautiful. Why had it taken him so long to notice? "What are your goals, Miss Foster?"

"My immediate goal is to find employment so I can reimburse the men who paid my passage here."

"And after that?"

"I am not one to make long-range goals, Mr. Jacobs. Only the Lord knows what tomorrow holds." Her huge green eyes searched his face. "What are your plans for the future, Mr. Jacobs?"

Adam's gaze shifted from her face to the distant mountain peaks. "My only goal was to be a physician." He sighed and turned to meet her questioning eyes. "When that didn't work out, I gave up on dreams."

"How sad."

He smiled wryly. "I probably wouldn't have made a very good doctor anyway."

"I am sure you would have been an excellent physician." Emily shoved her hands into the pockets of her coat. "However, that was not what I had reference to. Now, if you will excuse me, Mr. Jacobs, I will take my walk."

Adam watched her walk up the lane toward the main road. Despite the spring in her step, she looked alone. A strange feeling washed over him. Something he had never felt before. He wanted to take care of Emily. To take her hand in his and walk beside her through the uncharted waters that lay ahead.

His feelings stunned him, and he turned his thoughts and concerns to his Savior in a whispered prayer. "Lord, is this what love feels like? Surely not. I mean, it's probably just that she's so small and helpless looking. I don't want to do anything foolish like think I'm falling in love with her. I mean, after all, I don't even think she likes me much." That thought brought a stabbing pain in the vicinity of Adam's heart. "I'm putting this in Your hands, Lord. Not my will, but Thine be done, Father, in my life and in Emily's life."

As she walked up the lane, Emily rejoiced. Only God could have wrought such a change as she detected in Adam Jacobs. When she reached the main road, she turned and started back. Adam was standing where she had left him, his head bowed. Seeing him in an attitude of prayer, a feeling of tenderness stirred in her. A yearning toward him. *Is this how love feels?*

She came to a dead stop in the middle of the rutted lane. Where had such a foolish thought come from? She hardly knew Adam Jacobs. Besides, he barely tolerated her. She couldn't be the tiniest bit in love with him. Absolutely not! Why, she didn't even like him. She'd been praying for him, but only because her conscience compelled her to.

Oh, dear! That was the problem. How many times had Mama told her if you prayed for someone, you would come to love the one for whom you prayed? Of course, she meant as a brother or sister in Christ.

Isn't that so, Lord? My feelings for Mr. Jacobs are sisterly. Of course, I'm elated at him finding his way back to You. But that's all it is.

Her emotions regarding her brother in Christ clarified, Emily resumed her walk down the lane. As she drew near, Adam lifted his head and smiled. Then he walked toward the barn whistling a nameless melody.

Emily's heart did a flip-flop. *Lord, I don't think what I felt just now was the least bit sisterly. You have to get me out of here, Father. And soon!*

At breakfast, Emily concentrated on her plate as though scrambled eggs and biscuits were the most fascinating things in her life. Far more fascinating than Adam's brown eyes. She knew those brown eyes were looking at her. She sensed his gaze burning through the top of her head. If she looked up—if their eyes met across the table—he would see his own reflection in the green depths of her eyes. And she was afraid he might look all the way into her heart. She pushed the fluffy yellow and white eggs from one side of her plate to the other then back again.

"Emily." At the sound of Ruth's voice, she started and raised her head. Ruth's eyes were tender with concern. "Are you not feeling well, Emily?"

"No. I mean, yes. I'm fine. I guess I'm not hungry. May I please be excused?"

"Of course." Ruth frowned. "Are you sure you aren't ill?"

"Quite sure. I just. . .there is something I need to attend to."

"Oh, of course." Ruth's countenance cleared. "I understand. If you need anything, let me know."

Emily felt her face grow warm. Adam was a single man. He probably didn't know about female things, but John surely did. Besides, that wasn't her problem.

She fled to her bedroom, closed the door behind her, and threw herself across the neatly made bed. She had never been so confused in her life. Burying her face in the fluffy goose-down pillow, she let the tears flow.

Several minutes later, a gentle tap on the door, followed by Ruth calling her name, brought Emily to a sitting position.

"May I come in?"

"I guess so," she snuffled.

"Oh, Emily, you've been crying." Ruth crossed the room and sat down on the bed beside her. "What's wrong, honey? Maybe you would feel better if you talked about it."

The concern in Ruth's voice brought a fresh deluge of tears accompanied by wrenching sobs. Ruth put her arms around her and patted her back while Emily sobbed against her shoulder. Finally, when the tears were spent, Ruth released her and pressed a clean handkerchief into her hand.

"Want to tell me about it, honey?"

Emily wiped her eyes then blew her nose. "I know Mama is in heaven." She twisted the hanky between trembling hands. "I know she isn't blind anymore. Or sick."

Fresh tears filled her eyes. "I know it's selfish of me, Ruth, but I want my mother." She took a deep, sobbing breath. "Mama was my best friend. I need her, Ruth. I need her arms around me. I need her wise and loving counsel. I need her prayers. Most of all, I need her prayers. How will I survive without Mama to pray with me?"

"I know it wouldn't be the same." Ruth's blue eyes brimmed with compassionate tears. "But would you like me to pray with you?"

No, that was not what she wanted. It wouldn't be the same. Things would never again be the way they were before the fire. Emily wiped the tears from her face. But Ruth was a dear friend. Without a doubt, a friend sent by God for such a time as this. She reached out and clasped the young woman's hand. "I would be honored if you would pray with me."

Ruth's watery smile was a bit shaky. "Is there anything special we should pray about?"

"I would like to pray about my future. It's most important that I find employment soon if I wish to remain in Sanctuary. That's my main concern."

What about Adam?

Emily hesitated for a moment. She certainly didn't plan to share this morning's temporary loss of sanity with anyone. Least of all Adam Jacobs's sister-in-law. Precious as she was and much as she loved her, Ruth might misinterpret what even Emily didn't fully understand.

Adam Jacobs had nothing to do with her future. Absolutely. Positively. Nothing.

She clasped Ruth's hand. The two young women bowed their heads and began to pray. First, they prayed for Emily's situation. Then they prayed for Ruth's baby. Finally, Emily thanked God for bringing her to Sanctuary and allowing Ruth to come into her life. Ruth gave praise for Adam's restoration, and Emily's heart sang at the confirmation of what she had suspected earlier. Adam Jacobs had found his way home.

When the two young women uttered their final amen and looked at the clock, they saw almost an hour had passed. Laughing, they fell into each other's arms for one final hug. Then straightened Emily's bed and went to the kitchen.

"I thought we would bake bread today," Ruth said. "I already have the dough rising."

A pot of white beans simmered on the stove. The smell of warm yeast wafted from beneath the pristine white tea towel that covered the blue bowl sitting on top of the warming oven. Emily's empty stomach twisted. "It smells delicious."

"I saved your breakfast." Ruth removed a covered plate from the warming oven. "Do you feel like eating now?"

"Yes, thank you." She felt almost lighthearted as she took the plate from Ruth and sat down at the round oak table. "And thank you for praying with me, Ruth."

"We should pray together every morning."

"Yes, we should." *Except I won't be here many more mornings.* Emily bowed her head to offer a brief prayer of thanksgiving before eating her breakfast.

After her dishes were washed and put away, Emily moved to the baking table and made two raisin pies. While Ruth kneaded the bread dough, Emily washed the dishes she had used. By the time the dough was shaped into loaves and returned to the top of the warming oven, Emily was humming softly.

"I'm glad you are feeling better," Ruth ventured.

"So am I." Emily smiled. "Papa used to say, 'Earth hath no sorrow that heaven cannot heal.'"

"Your father must have been a very wise man."

Emily, her hands immersed in soapy dishwater, looked up. "He was. Papa was the most intelligent man I have ever known."

"Adam is quite intelligent."

"Yes, I am sure he is." Emily scrubbed at a stubborn spot on the pan she was washing.

"He is fond of you, Adam is. Did you know that?"

If Adam Jacobs was fond of her, he certainly had a strange way of showing it. Although he had been more civil the last few days, and this morning he had been almost friendly. "Ruth, I love you dearly, but I am not the least bit interested in your brother-in-law." Emily rinsed the pan and turned it upside down beside the sink to drain. "Nor does he care for me."

"You know, maybe we could go to prayer meeting tonight." A thoughtful expression crept into Ruth's blue eyes. "We don't usually, but the weather is good. I'll ask John."

"Do you think your father will have some news for me?"

"Perhaps." Ruth picked up the dish towel and began to dry the dishes Emily had washed. "There are several eligible bachelors in our church."

Emily laughed. "You are incorrigible, Ruth."

"Each of us has a God-given gift. Perhaps mine is match-making." Ruth grinned at Emily.

"And perhaps it isn't." Emily slipped a final pan into the rinse water. "Mama and I began praying for my future husband when

I was very young. When it is time, God will send that special someone into my life."

Emily took her hands from the soapy water and dried them. "I have always imagined how it will be. Our eyes will meet and my heart will skip a beat. And I'll know, Ruth. A small voice deep inside me will say he's the one."

Ruth's giggle caused Emily to blush. "I know it sounds silly, but in my dreams, it's incredibly sweet and beautiful."

"It is sweet and beautiful. It's only that you seem so practical. I never would have guessed you were a romantic at heart."

"Well"—Emily hung the dishtowel up to dry—"now I suppose you know everything there is to know about me."

"Wait until you meet my brother Matthew. If he doesn't cause your heart to skip a beat, no one will." Ruth patted Emily's shoulder. "Too bad Matt is already spoken for. I would so love to have you for a sister."

nine

That evening, Emily followed Ruth into the white clapboard church.

"Good evening, Sister Ruth." A dark-haired young man standing just inside the door shook Ruth's hand. "Isn't John with you?"

"John is seeing to the horses, and Adam is riding in."

"Adam will be present tonight. Wonderful." His blue eyes came to rest on Emily. "And this must be Adam's bride. I was told of your arrival in Sanctuary."

Emily felt the color rise in her face. "I fear you have been misinformed, sir. I am no one's bride."

Ruth put her arm around Emily's shoulders. "This is our pastor, Michael Barnes. Brother Michael, I would like you to meet my dear friend, Emily Foster."

The young minister took her hand in his. "I apologize for my misunderstanding. Welcome to Sanctuary, Miss Foster."

Emily gently withdrew her hand from his grasp.

"Emily is an accomplished pianist, Brother Michael," Ruth offered.

"Perhaps you would play for us, Miss Foster." The minister's blue eyes smiled at her. "We haven't had a regular pianist since Sister Jacobs passed away."

"Please say you will play," Ruth urged.

Emily's reluctance melted under the hopeful gaze of Ruth and the minister. "Do you have hymnals? If not, I can play by ear."

"Wonderful." The minister's enthusiasm shone from his

beaming face. "And, yes, we do have hymnals."

When he turned to greet some new arrivals, Ruth linked her arm with Emily's and led her around the room, introducing her to several people.

Adam still hadn't arrived when Emily took her place at the piano. Not that she cared. Mr. Jacobs's whereabouts were of absolutely no interest to her. None whatsoever. She was concerned about his well-being, of course. His horse could have thrown him. He could be lying beside the road with a broken leg. Or. . .

"Miss Emily Foster has agreed to play for us." Michael Barnes's voice interrupted her thoughts. "I'm sure most of you have already met Miss Foster. For those who haven't, Miss Foster is a friend of the Jacobs family. Now, for our first song, let us turn to page one hundred and six, 'He Leadeth Me.'"

Thoughts of Adam Jacobs faded to the back of Emily's mind as she lost herself in the words and music of the hymns she played. Twenty minutes later, when she turned from the piano, she saw Adam sitting with John and Ruth. She looked directly into his eyes and felt an unusual flutter in her chest. It was almost as though her heart had skipped a beat. Of course, that was nonsense. The quivering of her heart was merely relief that he was safe. It could be nothing else. Adam Jacobs bore no resemblance to the man she and Mama had prayed for.

She sat down on the first pew and looked down at her open Bible. Putting thoughts of Adam Jacobs aside, she turned her attention to the Bible study.

"Emily, my father wishes to speak with you." Ruth's voice was little more than a whisper against Emily's ear.

Emily's stomach tightened in nervous anticipation. "Has he found a position for me?"

"He only told me that he wants to talk to you now."

"Of course." Emily turned to the young woman she had been conversing with. "It was good to meet you, Sarah. Perhaps we can continue our conversation Sunday after church."

"That would be nice." Sarah Sloan smiled.

Ruth urged Emily toward a small group of men gathered at the back of the church with Mr. Reed. "Miss Foster, I'm happy you are here tonight. These gentlemen are interested in meeting you."

He introduced her to three older men before turning toward a younger man. "And this is my son Matthew."

Emily looked up into the bluest eyes she had ever seen. "Matt, Emily Foster, the young woman I have been telling you about."

"Miss Foster." Her hand was engulfed in a warm handshake. "I am very pleased to make your acquaintance."

Matthew Reed looked as though he might have stepped off a Viking ship. Tall. Muscular. Blond. And without doubt, the handsomest man she had ever seen. He released her hand. Emily caught her breath. "I'm pleased to meet you. Ruth has told me all about you."

"She has, has she?" He smiled with a grimace. "I hope she didn't really tell you *all* about me."

"I haven't yet." Ruth returned his smile. "But if you don't behave, I just may."

"All right, children," Mr. Reed interrupted, "save that for later."

"Miss Foster, my father says you studied to be a teacher." Matthew Reed's smile had vanished. He was all business. "Is that correct?"

"Yes, it is. But I never completed my education."

"What was your class standing?"

Emily hesitated. Should she tell him she had been at the

top of her class? Somehow that information, though true, seemed pretentious. "My grades were adequate."

"I'm sure they were." Matt exchanged glances with the other men before returning his attention to her. "I know this is a rather unusual place for a job interview. But under the circumstances, we thought the Lord would understand. We need a teacher for grades three and four, Miss Foster. Before we continue, are you interested in the position?"

Was she interested in the position? "I'm very interested, Mr. Reed. But as I explained to your father, I never received my degree."

"Miss Foster, my name is Watson," a small man wearing glasses introduced himself. "Bill Watson, president of the school board. Could you tell us if you have had any experience teaching children?"

Emily clasped her hands in front of her. "I taught Sunday school for several years."

"My wife's dead set on our Eva learning to play the piano." A tall, skinny man with a handlebar mustache, who had been introduced as the principal of Sanctuary's school, entered the conversation. "Could you teach her to play?"

"Yes, Mr. Ames. I can teach music."

After several more minutes of questions, the men exchanged glances. "Miss Foster, the job is yours if you want it," Bill Watson announced. "Can you start Monday morning?"

❧

At breakfast the next morning, Emily chattered more than she ate. This was a side of her personality Adam had never seen, and it intrigued him. She intrigued him. Why hadn't he realized that sooner?

"I still can't believe it." Her face glowed with happiness. "I'm going to be a teacher. Papa would be so proud."

"How do you think you will like working with Matt?"

"Your brother seems quite capable. I think I will enjoy working with him." Emily took a sip of coffee. "I understand your pastor also teaches in the high school. I have been intending to ask you if Brother Barnes is married."

"No, he isn't." Ruth leaned forward. "Brother Michael needs a helpmeet. You would make a wonderful pastor's wife, Emily."

Adam felt a sudden surge of jealousy. "Michael and Sarah Sloan are promised. I thought you knew that, Ruth."

"Goodness, Adam. While I'm certain they love one another deeply, they are practically brother and sister. The Sloans took Michael in when he was orphaned," Ruth explained to Emily. "Michael and Sarah were raised together."

"He was fifteen years old when his grandmother died." Adam scowled. "He carved a heart on his desk with Sarah's name in it."

"That was years ago." Ruth laughed. "You know, Emily. Puppy love."

"I spoke briefly with Sarah Sloan last night. She told me she teaches first and second grade." Emily sighed. "This all seems like a beautiful dream. You know I will be staying with the Sloans." She straightened in her chair. "Tell me about them, Ruth!"

"Mr. and Mrs. Sloan own the newspaper," Ruth began. "Sarah has an older brother named Ben. He's in the navy. . . ."

Emily and Ruth didn't even look up when Adam and John pushed back their chairs and walked out the door.

⁂

Saturday morning, Adam stowed Emily's battered valise in the boot of the buggy, then waited patiently while Ruth hugged Emily and extracted a promise that she would visit often.

Emily gave Ruth a final hug before Adam helped her onto the high seat of the buggy. She didn't say anything as they drove up the long lane to the main road. As the horses turned toward town, she released a ragged sigh and settled back in the seat.

Adam glanced at her. There was a glimmer of tears on her cheek. His heart yearned for her. Why had it taken him so long to realize how special she was?

He swallowed a lump in his throat. "Emily, there's something I have been meaning to ask you. I. . ." He felt as though he were drowning in those huge gold-flecked green eyes.

"What did you wish to ask, Mr. Jacobs?"

"I. . .uh. . ." He shook his head to clear it. "Would you please call me Adam?"

"I suppose that would be permissible, Mr. Jacobs." She smiled. "I mean, Adam."

Emily settled back in the seat. After a time, she said, "Isn't it amazing how things work out?"

Not waiting for him to reply, she continued. "I know it says in the Bible that all things work together for good to them who love the Lord, but it still amazes me how God can take the most unlikely circumstances and use them to fulfill His purpose."

She studied her hands, clasped tightly in her lap. "When I agreed to come here, I couldn't have realized that one of my fondest dreams would be fulfilled. But God did. He knew all along. Isn't He wonderful?"

Adam looked at her, his eyes betraying his skepticism. "Why would you think God was involved in something so depraved as what happened to you?"

"I faced a very bleak winter in the city with no income and no family to help me. I was praying that evening as I walked to my boardinghouse. I was terrified when those men snatched me off the street. I was sure they were going to kill me. When I discovered they planned something worse than death for me, I continued to pray, but I must admit, my faith wavered." She smiled. "Mr. Smith, the marriage broker, told me he had never attended a white slaver's auction before. But that morning, something compelled him to go. That's why I say God is wonderful. Don't you agree?"

"I agree that God is wonderful." Adam frowned. "Mr. Smith wasn't a Christian, was he?"

"No, but God used him anyway." Emily's green eyes sparkled. "I had a chance to witness to him on the way to the train, Adam. He said his mother had been a fine Christian woman and he had been raised in the church. As he grew older, he turned away from God. I pray for him every day."

"How can you pray for a man like that? Aren't you angry at what happened to you?"

"Angry at whom, Adam?" Her green eyes searched his face. "God? Or Mr. Smith?"

Her serious gaze made Adam uncomfortable. "The men who snatched you off the street and the Smith fellow, I suppose."

"How could I be angry at them? They were only unwitting instruments in the hands of my heavenly Father. The Father takes care of us even when we don't realize it."

She turned away from him and began to sing softly. "In shady green pastures, so rich and so sweet, God leads His dear children along."

After a bit, Adam joined in. Long before he was ready for their trip to end, he brought the buggy to a stop in front of a white frame house on the edge of town.

ten

"This was my brother's room." Sarah stepped aside to let Emily enter the room ahead of her. "I know it's a bit masculine, but there wasn't time to redecorate. Besides, Mother said we should let you change things to suit yourself."

Emily looked around the cozy room with wide-eyed interest. The furnishings were heavy and dark. A log cabin quilt, pieced in dark blue and red plaid, covered the bed. Navy blue plaid drapes hung at the two windows. It wasn't decorated to her taste, but the room was immaculate, and she was grateful to have a place she could call her own.

"It's fine, Sarah." She dropped her bag on the bed. "I wouldn't dream of changing a thing."

"There's no reason you shouldn't change it." Sarah sat down on the edge of the bed. "Ben will never stay here again."

"I'm sorry." A flush touched Emily's cheeks. "Evidently, Ruth doesn't know. She told me. . ."

"Oh, you don't think my brother's dead, do you?" Sarah laughed. "I'm sorry if I gave that impression. No, Ben isn't dead, Emily, just off sailing the high seas. A year or so ago, he announced his intention to join the navy. Can you imagine? He had never even seen an ocean. Anyway, the next thing we knew, he was gone. He writes occasionally, though not nearly as much as Mother would like him to."

Sarah shrugged. "He seems to like it. The navy, I mean. He says he's going to make a career of it. Can you imagine seeing nothing but water for months at a time? No trees. Or grass. Nothing but water. I couldn't endure it."

It would be difficult, but over the last few months, Emily had learned you could endure almost anything if you had to.

She looked around the room again. Maybe she would make a few changes as she could afford them. Frilly white curtains and a more colorful quilt would brighten the room considerably.

"Mother has some white muslin that would make curtains," Sarah said. "And I have a double wedding ring quilt in my hope chest that would be perfect in here."

"Sarah, I couldn't take your quilt. You will want it someday."

"It doesn't seem likely I'll ever need it." Sarah's smile didn't make it to her eyes. "I could put all my hopes in a matchbox."

❦

After dropping Emily off, Adam stopped in town to pick up a few things for Ruth, then headed back to the ranch. He stopped near the back porch of the house and carried Ruth's things in.

Ruth turned from the stove. "Did you get Emily to the Sloans?"

He nodded and piled his parcels on the kitchen table.

Ruth sighed. "The house already seems empty without her."

"Yeah, well, we'll soon get used to her being gone."

"We?" Ruth smiled.

"You." Adam spoke quickly. "By the way, where is John?"

"He went over to the Thompsons'. Ike stopped by and said they needed some help. I don't think he'll be gone long."

"Probably not." He stepped to the door. "Guess I'll take Copper out and look for strays."

"I thought you and John already—" Ruth stopped in mid-sentence and handed him two molasses cookies. "Take these with you, Adam. They're still warm."

"Thanks." Adam put the cookies in his pocket. "I'll be back by suppertime."

"Adam."

His hand on the doorknob, he turned to face his sister-in-law.

"Lewis has been a faithful friend. Don't you think it's time to forgive him?"

Adam stared down at his boots for a moment, then, without giving a direct answer, said, "I'll be back before dark."

At the barn, he unhitched the buggy and took care of the horse before heading for Copper's stall. "How about we go out looking for strays?"

Cooper didn't appear too interested. Well, that was understandable. Even Ruth had known there were no strays. They had brought the last of them in from the Thompson brothers' place a few days after Emily's arrival.

He had thought riding over the ranch, looking for non-existent strays, would take his mind off something that had been bothering him since the night he found his way back to God. But he was wrong.

Lewis Thompson had been his best friend for as long as he could remember. When he came home after his father's death, it had been Lewis who met him at the train. Lewis was at his side when Dr. Brown came out of the bedroom and told them his mother was gone. Though he never said much, Lewis's quiet presence and willing ear had comforted him during the greatest sorrows of his life.

A stiff wind from the northwest chilled his face. Looked like they might be in for another storm. The last blizzard had brought Emily. Emily with her torn wrists and forgiving heart.

He turned Copper toward home. Lewis had never knowingly done him harm. He would willingly give his life for him. Adam knew this as surely as he knew he'd never find peace until he patched things up with his friend.

"Next time I see Lewis, I'm going to ask his forgiveness." The wind snatched the words and flung them from him. He pulled his cap over his ears and hunkered down in the saddle.

It was snowing when he rode into the barn. John came in as he was leaving.

"Think we need to string up the rope?"

"Wouldn't hurt."

"You better spend the night with us."

Adam nodded his agreement and followed John into the biting cold. They secured the rope, then fed it out behind them as they made their way to the house.

☙

Emily woke early Sunday morning. Throwing the covers aside, she raced across the room to the ice-encrusted window. The sun, peeking over the eastern horizon, sparkled on the thin blanket of snow, turning the ground into a field of diamonds. It was going to be a beautiful day. She hugged herself in delight. *Thank You, Lord!* She made the bed then dressed for church.

The buggy ride was short, but she welcomed the warmth of the Sanctuary Community Church. Brother Michael waited just inside the front door to greet his flock. After exchanging pleasantries with Mr. and Mrs. Sloan, he took Sarah's hand in his. If Adam hadn't mentioned that they were in love, Emily doubted she would even have noticed the change that came over the young woman's countenance. Sarah's blue eyes deepened, and her face took on a radiance that could only be attributed to one thing. Her mother had worn that same expression when Emily's father held her hand. Yes, despite Ruth's insistence that Michael Barnes and Sarah Sloan were merely childhood friends, it was obvious they were much more.

The young minister released Sarah's hand and turned to Emily. "Are you excited about starting school tomorrow, Miss Foster?"

"I'm very excited, Brother Barnes."

A gust of cold air swept in with the next arrivals. The Sloans moved on, and Emily followed them, but not before she saw John and Ruth step through the door followed by Adam.

Emily hesitated, uncertain whether she should go with the Sloans or wait to speak with Ruth. While she was trying to decide, Ruth left the men and approached her.

"Emily, you can't imagine how much I miss you." She glanced over her shoulder. John had moved on, but Adam appeared to be involved in a serious discussion with the minister. "We all miss you."

"I miss you, too, Ruth." Her gaze came to rest on Adam before returning to Ruth. "I miss all of you."

"We're looking forward to you visiting the ranch often."

Two couples and a small child entered the church on a blast of frigid air. The taller of the two men hesitated just inside the doorway, while the rest of his group stepped forward to greet the pastor. Brother Michael shook their hands and greeted them with his customary, "How are the Thompsons today?"

Adam had stepped aside and was exchanging glances with the man standing in the door.

"Are these the men who sent for me?" Emily asked.

Ruth, her attention on her brother-in-law, nodded.

"I need to speak to them."

Ruth laid a hand on her arm. "Not now."

The older couple moved on with their child. Emily saw the minister's gaze move from the plump blond girl with whom he was conversing to Adam, then to the man standing alone in the shadows.

Adam squared his shoulders and moved to stand in front of the other man.

"Oh, dear," Ruth murmured.

"Is that Lewis Thompson?" Emily whispered.

"Yes, and. . ." Ruth nodded. "Oh, dear," she repeated as the two men moved to the corner of the room. "Perhaps I should get John."

"They wouldn't fight, would they? I mean, not in church." Emily watched wide-eyed as the two men talked. Or Adam talked. Lewis Thompson listened. Then a broad smile crept across his homely face. She breathed a sigh of relief. Perhaps they weren't going to come to blows after all.

Lewis punched Adam on the shoulder with his closed fist. Adam punched Lewis back.

Emily gasped. "We must stop them, Ruth."

When she moved to dash to Adam's assistance, Ruth's hand restrained her. "It's all right, Emily." Ruth chuckled. "They're making up."

"Making up?" By this time, they had exchanged two more blows. "You're mistaken, Ruth. We mustn't allow them to engage in fisticuffs in the Lord's house."

"See!" Ruth smiled. "It's all over."

Adam followed Lewis to where the rest of the Thompson family sat. He nodded a greeting to them before sitting down beside Lewis.

"I don't understand," Emily said. "If they were settling their differences, why were they pounding on each other?"

"That's the way Adam and Lewis are." Ruth laughed. "They've been best friends forever. They have always done that. To them it's the same as a hug would be to you or me. You know, a display of affection. All men are like that."

"I guess I don't know much about men," Emily said. "But beating on someone seems a most unusual way to show affection."

Before Ruth had a chance to reply, someone spoke Emily's

name. She turned to look up at the minister. "You will play the piano for us again, won't you?"

Emily smiled. "I would be honored, Brother Barnes."

Church that morning was food for the soul. Or at least Emily thought so. Brother Michael preached an inspiring message on walking by faith. The songs they sang uplifted her soul as she played and listened to the congregation's enthusiastic voices as they praised God. After the service, the people she met welcomed her with friendly smiles and handshakes. She spoke briefly with Adam, and if her heart jumped with an extra surge of joy when she looked up into his chocolate brown eyes, she attributed it to her overall feeling of well-being. For the first time since the fire, she felt as though she truly belonged somewhere. She wasn't merely a sojourner in Sanctuary. God had led her home.

eleven

Sunday afternoon, the Sloan family retreated to their separate rooms to rest. In her room, Emily selected a book from Ben Sloan's collection and settled down to read. Before she opened the cover, Sarah tapped on the facing of the open door.

"I thought you might like to visit," she said.

"Yes, I would like that." Emily laid the book, *A Tale of Two Cities*, to one side and settled back in the armchair.

Sarah pulled the chair around from the desk to face her and sat down. "How did you like church?"

"I enjoyed the service very much."

"What about the sermon? Did you think it was good?"

"Very inspiring." Emily smiled.

Sarah worked at an imaginary hangnail. "How do you like Brother Michael?"

"I found him to be a gifted speaker."

"Oh, he is!" Sarah looked up, her face aglow. "He's very intelligent and a dedicated Bible scholar."

"Yes, I can see that." Emily pulled the woolen shawl from the back of the chair and wrapped it around her shoulders. "How long have you been in love with Brother Barnes, Sarah?"

"Oh, no, I didn't mean. . ." Sarah looked down at her clasped hands for a moment before raising tear-filled eyes. "I don't remember when I didn't love Michael."

Emily remained silent, waiting.

"He doesn't share my feelings." Sarah's sigh quavered with unshed tears. "He sees me as Ben's little sister, nothing more."

Emily had detected something deeper in the young minister's expression when he spoke to Sarah. "I feel you are mistaken," she said. "There is a special tenderness in his eyes when he looks at you."

"Oh, Michael loves me," Sarah said. "He just isn't in love with me. He thinks of me as a younger sister. You see——" She took a folded quilt from the foot of the bed and wrapped it around her before sitting back down. "Michael lost his parents when he was a little boy. After that, he came to Montana to live with his grandparents. They passed away when he was a young teenager, and he came to live with us. Ben and Michael had been friends since he moved in with his grandparents; after he came here, they were inseparable."

Sarah adjusted the blanket around her shoulders. "I followed them everywhere. Ben made no secret of the fact that he considered me a nuisance. Michael probably did, too, but he was always patient and kind. Have you ever been in love, Emily?"

The unexpected question caught her off guard. Adam Jacobs's face passed through her mind. "No," she said, shaking her head, "I never have."

"I know—well, probably everyone in Sanctuary knows—you came here to marry Adam, and I was wondering. . . Well, don't you find him attractive?"

The image Emily often had to shove from her mind reappeared—the first time she had seen Adam shaved and clean and standing in the Jacobses' kitchen. She had been shocked to find such a handsome man under that atrocious beard he had worn as a mask. She swallowed before answering.

"Yes, I do find Adam Jacobs attractive, but I had no intention of marrying him when I came west. Perhaps when we become better acquainted, I shall tell you why I came to Sanctuary." Emily's voice sounded soft in the silent room.

"It's a long—and very personal—story."

"Oh, Emily, please forgive me." Sarah's voice reflected the distress in her face. "I am so sorry. I was completely out of line."

"It's all right." Emily took Sarah's hand. "I suppose I'm a bit sensitive when it comes to Adam Jacobs and the whole subject of mail-order brides."

"I should never have asked you such a personal question." Tears pooled in Sarah's blue eyes. "I so want us to be friends."

"And I am sure we shall be." Emily smiled as she released the young woman's hand.

"It's just that—" The tears overflowed Sarah's eyes. "You're beautiful and refined; you can sing and play the piano. I am none of those things, and I have no musical talent. I can't even carry a tune. You're wonderful, Emily."

"It's nice of you to say those things." Whatever was Sarah talking about? "But I'm really quite ordinary."

"You aren't ordinary at all, but I am." Sarah brushed at her wet cheeks with the back of her hand. "It has always been my greatest fear that someone like you would come along and win Michael's heart. You would make a perfect minister's wife."

"What!" Emily couldn't suppress an incredulous laugh. "I have no romantic feelings for Brother Barnes, Sarah. Nor, I'm certain, does he view me as anything more than a member of his flock."

"But you said he was a gifted speaker and his message was inspirational."

"He is, and it was. I came from a large city, Sarah. I have heard many gifted speakers and even more inspiring messages. I didn't set my cap for any of those men. I'm not looking for a husband."

"Never?" Sarah's eyes were round. "Don't you want to marry and have a family?"

"Of course I would like that." Emily sighed. "If marriage is God's will for me, then someday He will bring the person He has chosen into my life." The image of Adam's lopsided grin intruded on her thoughts. She quickly pushed it aside. "Until then, I am content."

"Let's go to the kitchen where it's warmer." Sarah cast aside the quilt. "We can make hot cocoa and pop some corn."

"All right." Emily folded the shawl and returned it to the back of the chair before replacing the book on the shelf.

"I can tell you all about our school."

"I would like that." Emily arranged the quilt at the foot of the bed, then she followed Sarah to the kitchen.

ఌ

The following morning, when Sarah and Emily arrived at the school, several students waited in small groups on the snow-patched lawn. Brother Michael came out the front door as they entered the building.

"Good morning, ladies." He smiled. "Ready for your big day, Miss Foster?"

"I hope so," Emily replied.

"Just remember, it gets easier with time." He bounded down the front steps. An ear-splitting whistle shattered the silence.

"What on earth!" Emily gasped.

"That was Michael's whistle," Sarah explained. "He's leading calisthenics this morning."

"It's certainly shrill, isn't it?"

"Ben gave it to him for Christmas one year. Sometimes I have been sorely tempted to cram it down his throat."

"Really?" Emily looked at the other girl with feigned astonishment. "I can't imagine you feeling that way about your pastor."

"I didn't say he was perfect." Sarah giggled. "But he comes close. As a matter of fact, if it weren't for that whistle. . ."

Sarah stopped in front of an open door. "This is it, Emily. Would you like me to show you around before the thundering herd arrives?"

"I would appreciate that. I'm a bit nervous."

"You will do fine." Sarah gave her arm a reassuring pat before walking to the front of the room and opening the lap drawer of the desk. She removed a thin, gray book and handed it to Emily. "This is your attendance and grade book. All your students' names are in here. Miss Gates has them seated in alphabetical order. Keep this book on your desk, and if you forget someone's name, you can find it here."

"Thank you, Sarah."

"You're welcome." Sarah gave her a brief hug. "If you need anything, I'll be right next door."

Emily accompanied Sarah to the door, then stood aside as the children began to file into the room.

When the last child had entered, she closed the door and moved to the front of the room. She stood facing her class. Her class! How wonderful that sounded even in her mind. "Good morning, children."

"Good morning," they answered in singsong voices.

"I am Miss Foster, your new teacher." She retrieved the attendance book from the desk. "Please raise your hand when I call your name. Melissa Abbot."

A small girl with red braids raised her hand. Emily read the next name. She smiled at the children as she carefully committed each name and face to memory.

"Frank Young." She read the final name and closed the book.

Moving to her desk, she picked up her Bible and read a passage from Psalms. After a short prayer, she stood behind the desk and faced her class.

"As I said before, my name is Miss Foster. Miss Emily

Foster. I am from New York City. On July 26, 1788, New York ratified the Constitution and became the eleventh state to join the Union. Today, November eighth, is an important anniversary for the state of Montana. Can anyone tell me what happened in Montana on this date in 1889?"

A hand in the last row shot up. Dark hair and a scattering of freckles. Thomas Wilson. Emily smiled. "Yes, Thomas."

"Montana became a state."

"Very good."

"My state was the eleventh colony to declare statehood. Can anyone tell me in what order Montana was admitted to the Union?"

The hand in the last row was waving. "Yes, Thomas."

"We were the forty-first state admitted to the Union."

"That is correct." Emily smiled at her eager student. "Can any of you tell me why your family came west?"

This time no one raised a hand.

Emily stepped to the side of her desk and explained, "Most of the state of Montana was part of the Louisiana Purchase. At different times, parts of Montana were territories of Washington, Idaho, Missouri, Dakota, Oregon, Louisiana, and Nebraska. In 1862, gold was discovered in southwestern Montana. Many of the early settlers came in search of gold. At that time, Montana was part of the Idaho Territory. In December of 1864, the Montana Territory was created."

Emily walked around her desk. "I think it might be interesting if you talked to your parents. Ask them how they came to settle in Montana. Find out if your family traveled the Oregon Trail."

The children seemed interested in what she had to say. An idea began to take shape in Emily's head. "Raise your hand if you would like to put together a book on the settlement of Sanctuary."

Every hand in the room was raised. "All right." Emily felt her own excitement growing. "I want you to talk to as many people as you can. Not only your parents or grandparents, but aunts, uncles, and the older settlers. Gather as much information as possible, then I want each of you to write a paper on what you have learned. We will take your stories and compile a book."

The hand in the last row waved. "Yes, Thomas?"

"When is the assignment due, Miss Foster?"

Emily hesitated. She didn't want to rush them. "The third week of January. That will give you time to collect your material. Now, if you will take out your arithmetic books."

An hour later, Emily hugged her coat close as she watched the children dash around the schoolyard playing Blind Man's Bluff.

"How has your morning gone so far?" Sarah came to stand beside her.

"Fast," Emily replied with a smile.

"Did Thomas answer all the questions?"

"He tried to."

"He's very bright." Sarah cupped her hands around her mouth. "No shoving, Samuel." She stuck her hands in her pockets. "His mother says he started reading before he was three years old. She may have embroidered on the truth a smidgen, but I do know he's read every book we have here at school."

Emily thought of the few books in her classroom. If they were any example, the selection of reading material was meager in the Sanctuary school.

The second half of the morning passed even more swiftly than the first. Most of Emily's pupils walked home for lunch. The remaining children retrieved their lunches from the shelf at the back of the room and sat at their desks eating. Emily stayed at her own desk eating the sandwich she had prepared that morning. Her companions cast furtive glances in her direction. Though she smiled, most of them ducked their heads and concentrated on their cold meal.

That afternoon, Emily sat facing the children. "I thought I would read to you for thirty minutes each afternoon, before we start classes. Would you like that?"

Most of the children nodded. Emily smiled and picked up the book she had borrowed from Ben Sloan's library. She had debated bringing this book to read to her third- and fourth-grade pupils—feeling they might not understand it.

"This is a book by Mr. Charles Dickens—a well-known English author. The title is *A Tale of Two Cities*. My father read it aloud to me when I was about your age, and I enjoyed it very much. I thought you might, too."

She opened the book. " 'Chapter one. The Period. It was the best of times, it was the worst of times, it was the age of wisdom, it was the age of foolishness, it was the epoch of belief, it was the epoch of incredulity, it was the season of Light, it was the season of Darkness. . . .' "

The children sat entranced until she closed the book at the end of the third chapter. They had such a thirst for knowledge. There must be some way to obtain more books for these children. Emily sighed.

"Charles Dickens was writing about the French Revolution. In our own country, we fought for freedom from England. Can anyone tell me what started the American Revolution?"

Emily ignored Thomas's waving hand. "Yes, Eva."

The small blond girl hesitated for a moment. "The Boston Tea Party?"

"Yes." Emily smiled at her. "But there was something else. Yes, Thomas."

"Taxation without representation." His blue eyes reflected his excitement. "The colonists dressed up like Indians and threw the tea into Boston Harbor because they thought the taxes on it were unfair."

"Very good." Emily smiled as other hands were raised.

The afternoon passed even more swiftly than the morning. After dismissing her students, Emily straightened the room and gathered her coat and book bag.

"So how did it go?" Emily looked up as Matthew Reed strode through the door.

"Quite well," Emily replied with a smile. "At least I think it did."

"Are you ready to go, Emily?" Sarah breezed through the door. "Good afternoon, Matthew."

Before he could respond, Brother Michael stepped into the room, accompanied by a slender, scholarly-looking man he introduced as Charles Wise. "Charles and I thought we would see if you ladies would like an escort home."

twelve

Adam nudged Copper forward as he came in sight of the large brick building where Emily had spent the day. If the kids he saw walking along the street were any indication, school had already been dismissed. Teachers usually stayed a few minutes after the last child left. Surely, she was still there.

If he could have slipped the buggy past Ruth's eagle eyes, he could have seen Emily home in style. As it was, they would have to walk. Emily had been gone three days, and although he would never admit it to anyone—least of all his matchmaking sister-in-law—Emily's leaving had left an empty place in his life. No matter how busy he was, she was never far from his thoughts. He had convinced himself if he could see her, talk to her just one more time, he could put her out of his mind.

Adam shook his head. Nothing would ever be the same after Emily. Her large green eyes would haunt him the rest of his life.

He was almost half a block away when he saw Emily and Sarah Sloan step out the front door of the schoolhouse. Michael Barnes and a man he didn't recognize followed them and fell into step on each side of the two young women.

Adam pulled Copper to a stop at the side of the road and sat watching the foursome approach. Emily looked up at the slender stranger at her side. Red-hot pain sliced through Adam's heart.

He turned and rode back the way he had come. There

was only one explanation for the ache in his chest. He loved Emily Foster. Nothing less could hurt so much.

"Isn't that Adam Jacobs?" Sarah asked. "I didn't see him go past, did you?"

Emily immediately recognized the proud set of Adam's shoulders as he rode away from them. For a moment, her heart seemed to stop before rushing on. "Why would Adam Jacobs be riding past the school at this time of day?"

Sarah nudged Emily with her elbow. "Maybe he hoped to catch a glimpse of a certain young teacher."

Michael chuckled. "So there is a grain of truth to those rumors."

"Oh, honestly!" Emily shook her head, deciding to do some teasing of her own. "Of course there isn't. But what of you two? You've been friends for a long time, haven't you?"

Michael squeezed Sarah's shoulders. "We have been friends forever, haven't we, Sukie?"

"Sukie?" Charles Wise and Emily said in unison.

"That's what Michael and Ben called me when I was younger." She dug an elbow into Michael's ribs. "I hated it then, and I despise it now."

Charles Wise chose to change the subject. "Is it true that you will be teaching music, Miss Foster?"

"Yes." Emily smiled at the serious young man. "My mother taught music before she married my father. She was an accomplished pianist. I only hope I shall do half as well."

"You will," Michael said. "To my knowledge, you are the best pianist we've had in our church. I know you are the best I have ever heard. I want to thank you for your invaluable contribution to our services."

"I don't know what to say." Emily blushed at his praise. "I enjoy playing, and I am happy to be able to make a contribution."

"He's right, you are very good," Sarah spoke up. "However,

I would advise you to be very careful, Emily. I know Michael, and I know what he is leading up to."

"You think so, do you?" Michael grasped the nape of Sarah's neck and gave her a gentle shake. "You don't know everything, Sukie."

"Maybe not." Sarah laughed as she moved out of his reach. "But I know you."

"I was only thinking that Miss Foster is the perfect person to direct our Christmas program this year." He grinned at Sarah. "With your able assistance, of course."

"Me?" Sarah put a hand to her throat. "Who says I'm going to get involved this year?"

"I do." The twinkle in Michael's eyes belied his stern look. "It's good training for you, little girl."

"Training?" Sarah's expression became serious. "And what is it I am supposed to be training for, Michael?"

"God has a plan for each of us, Sarah." Michael's expression was as solemn as Sarah's. "We never know what He has in store for us, but we need to be prepared."

"That sounds like Christian double-talk to me." Charles Wise's voice reflected his disdain. "I know you are a minister, Barnes, but surely you don't believe that nonsense."

"If I didn't believe it, I wouldn't be much of a shepherd, would I?"

"What do you believe, Mr. Wise?" Emily asked.

"I believe man is master of his own destiny." The man looked as if he were prepared to deliver an oration. "It is my belief that man is born, lives a few short years, then dies."

"Then what happens to him?" Sarah asked.

"Why, eventually he becomes dust. I am a moral person, Miss Sloan. I do not carouse or smoke or curse. I live my life as uprightly as any Christian does. I do what I feel to be right. I harm no one. I live a righteous life."

Emily quoted from Proverbs. " 'There is a way which see-meth right unto a man, but the end thereof are the ways of death.' "

"Quite so, Miss Foster." Charles Wise smiled. "Isn't that what I just said? Each of us is going to die."

"I don't wish to argue with you, Mr. Wise," Emily said. "I'm quite sure nothing I say will change your mind."

"Miss Foster. Charles. You are both new here." Michael smiled. "Are you aware that we have a fellowship dinner at church the Saturday evening before Thanksgiving?"

Emily was thankful Michael had drawn the conversation away from Charles and his beliefs. "I have heard about it," she said. "And I am planning to attend. What about you, Mr. Wise?"

"I think not," he replied. "I don't relish an evening of being preached to."

"For that you will have to come to Sunday service." Michael's countenance was serious. "No one will preach to you next Saturday evening, Charles."

"All right. I'll think about it," the young man said.

"Good!" Michael smiled. "And you are welcome to attend church services anytime you wish."

"I don't need to think about that," Charles said. "The answer is no. I will never again darken a church house doorway."

They talked about other things on the remainder of the short walk. Emily did not like Charles Wise, but she purposed in her heart to pray for him every day and to be his friend.

❧

"Sarah, it's obvious that Michael Barnes is in love with you." Emily tilted her head and looked thoughtful. "But I don't believe he realizes it."

Sarah sat on the bed in Emily's room, watching her with wide blue eyes. "Of course he doesn't. You saw how he treats me." She bowed her head. "Thanks for trying to cheer me up, Emily, but Michael loves me just like any big brother would."

"No, he doesn't." Emily frowned. "And somehow we're going to make him recognize his true feelings."

Emily paced the room, ignoring Sarah's protesting noises. Michael and Sarah belonged together. As the pastor of the largest church in Sanctuary, Michael needed a wife. He needed Sarah. Suddenly, she stopped pacing and snapped her fingers.

"I have it."

"You have what?"

"Sarah, are there any unmarried men in the church besides Matthew?"

Sarah grinned. "Sure, there's Adam."

Emily's expression must have mirrored her consternation, because Sarah laughed.

"I thought so." Sarah pointed at Emily. "You know as well as I do that Adam was outside the schoolhouse today because he wanted to see you. The men must have scared him off. He probably thought you were with Charles Wise."

When Emily remained quiet, Sarah grew thoughtful. "I know what you have in mind, but do you think it would work, Emily? I don't want to use some unsuspecting man just to make Michael jealous, but if I thought it would work, I might consider it."

"Yes, I think it would work." Emily, glad to think of something besides Adam, sat on the bed beside Sarah. "But you are right. We can't use another person who might get hurt."

"Especially not Adam, huh?" The teasing light was back in Sarah's eyes.

Emily's smile held a touch of sadness. "No, not anyone. It wouldn't be right, Sarah. My father always said, 'Deceit is the false road to happiness.'"

"Your father was right." Sarah turned away from Emily for a moment. When she looked back, her expression held so much sadness, Emily felt like crying. "I've prayed and prayed."

"When you prayed, did you leave your burden with the Lord?" Emily's voice was gentle. "Or did you put it back on your own shoulders and carry it away with you as we so often do? And, Sarah, have you asked God if there's anything you can do about your situation?"

"Do? What can I do?"

"How about talking to Michael?"

Sarah doubled her fist and hit her knee. "Sometimes I'd like to walk up to him and tell him exactly what I think." She slumped into the posture of defeat. "But I'm afraid if I do, it will scare him away."

"Let's pray, Sarah." Emily slipped to her knees beside the bed. "Let's pray right now that God will direct you and Michael. Pray for the opportunity to speak your mind, if that's what God directs, or even just for Michael to wake up and see you as you are. Don't try to muddle through by yourself, but be sensitive to God's leading. . . ."

"All right." A slow smile lit Sarah's face as she knelt beside Emily. " 'I can do all things through Christ who strengtheneth me.' Even win Michael's heart."

"If it is the Lord's will," Emily added softly.

Sarah nodded. "This time I'm going to leave my burden with the Lord."

❧

Emily didn't encourage Charles Wise's friendship, but she tried to be pleasant and friendly when he sought her out. Which turned out to be more often than she would have liked. Her faith was the most important thing in life to her. As far as she could tell, Charles was an atheist. At the very least, he was not the sort of gentleman with whom she wished to become romantically involved. Much as Emily disliked Charles, she continued to pray for the arrogant young man.

Adam Jacobs continually hovered near the fringes of her thoughts. One evening, in the privacy of Sarah's bedroom, she asked her friend about Gertrude.

"Gertrude Phillips is my cousin. She likes to be called Trudy. She says it sounds more modern." Sarah sighed. "A little over a year ago, Aunt Bethene sent her to us. Gertrude had become involved with an unsuitable man, and my aunt thought she would forget him if she put enough distance between the two of them."

"So she fell in love with Mr. Jacobs?" Emily asked.

"I doubt Trudy has ever loved anyone except herself." Sarah pulled the pins from her hair. "My cousin is an outrageous flirt. Adam was merely a diversion for her. A month after they met, they were betrothed. Two months later, Trudy's lover from Chicago found her—I'm certain she wrote him—and the two of them left town together."

"She left without a word?" Emily tried to imagine how Adam must have felt.

"Oh, no!" Sarah pulled a brush through her long blond hair. "She entrusted me to deliver a letter to Adam." A tinge of pink touched her cheeks. "I know it was wrong, but I read it. Then I burned it. She said terrible things, Emily. Demeaning, mocking things. I didn't want her to inflict more pain on Adam than she already had. Maybe I should have given him her letter, but—"

"No!" Emily's heart ached for Adam Jacobs. "Reading such a letter would have only hurt him more."

"Anyway," Sarah said, smiling, "he is finally over Trudy. Adam Jacobs has given his heart to you, my friend."

"Mr. Jacobs's heart appears to be easily given." Emily took the brush from her friend's hand and began to brush Sarah's long blond tresses. "I think it might be unwise to fall in love with such a man."

"But you already have." Sarah's blue eyes teased. "You love Adam, don't you?"

"I have never been in love. I am not sure I recognize the symptoms." Her nose burned as she fought to hold back the tears. "Oh, Sarah, I fear you are correct. I do love Adam."

Sarah clapped her hands. "How wonderful. You love him. He loves you. What could be more perfect?"

"It would be perfect if not for Gertrude's memory." Emily couldn't bring herself to call Adam's first love by her nickname. "How could I ever compete with a dream, Sarah? Even if things worked out between the two of us—" Emily blushed. "Even if we married and had children together, she would always occupy a special place in Adam's heart."

"Five years from now, Adam won't even remember her name, Emily." Sarah scoffed. "He never loved her in the first place. It was merely an infatuation. Michael says his pride was wounded more than his heart when she ran away."

"Speaking of Pastor Barnes." Emily smiled at her friend's reflection in the mirror. "He seems more attentive of late."

"Not attentive enough." Sarah flipped her hair over her shoulder and began to braid it. "At the rate things are moving, I'll be too old to walk down the aisle by the time he notices I've grown up. Aunt Bethene has been begging me to come to Chicago. Maybe I should accept her invitation and leave Michael to stew in his own juices."

Sarah secured the end of her braid and stood. "Speaking of attentive gentleman. . ." The teasing light was back in her eyes. "What about you and Mr. Wise? He follows you around like a lovesick puppy."

"I don't know why." Emily didn't bother to argue the obvious. "Except for being raised in New York State, we have nothing in common. The man's philosophy repulses me. He informed me today that he was an adherent to Charles Darwin's theory of evolution through natural selection."

"The man's an evolutionist?" Sarah gasped. "Do you think the school board knows?"

"Probably not. Otherwise they wouldn't have hired him." Emily sat down on the edge of Sarah's bed. "He offered to loan me a copy of *The Descent of Man*."

"Isn't that the book where Darwin expounds the theory that man is descended from chimpanzees or some such nonsense?" Sarah sat on the bed beside Emily. "What did you say?"

"I refused, of course." Emily sighed. "He asked me to accompany him to the Thanksgiving dinner at church."

"You aren't going to do it, are you?"

"I told him I would."

"Oh, Emily, why?"

"I know Brother Michael has been inviting him to church—"

"And he has been steadfastly refusing."

"Yes, I know. But I thought if Mr. Wise met the people from church—got acquainted with them—he might change his mind."

"Aren't you afraid that he may think you are interested in him?" Sarah wrinkled her nose. "You know. In a romantic way."

"That is why I thought we could all go together. You, Brother Michael, Mr. Wise, and myself."

"But I'm not going with Michael."

"Yes, you are." Emily laughed. "I have already discussed it with Brother Michael. He has agreed to meet us at the church on Saturday night."

thirteen

When Emily walked through the fellowship hall door with the same man he had seen her with in front of the school, Adam's heart sank. Her gaze met his for the briefest moment before coming to rest on Ruth. She made her way across the crowded room to hug his sister-in-law. Then she took her place at the piano and began to play.

Adam studied the man she came with. Short, slight, and fair-haired, he wore gold-rimmed glasses. What did Emily see in him? He crossed the room to Sarah and the two men.

"Adam, it's good to see you." Michael clasped his hand in a brief handshake. "I don't believe you have met our mathematics teacher. Adam Jacobs, this is Charles Wise."

"Mr. Wise was raised in New York, also," Sarah added. "He and Emily are finding they have much in common."

What could Emily have in common with this dandified little pipsqueak? "I don't believe I have seen you in church, Mr. Wise."

"And you never shall." The little man's lip curled beneath an all but invisible mustache. "I don't require a deity to keep watch over my life. I believe man is in charge of his own destiny."

"In that case, I'd say you are in big trouble, buddy." Adam did not like this man. He wasn't fit to polish Emily's shoes. "I would advise you to stay away from Miss Foster."

"As far as I know, Miss Foster is a free woman. She can choose with whom she wishes to spend her time." He drew himself up to his full five-feet-six-inches to glare up at Adam. "And she has chosen me."

"We will just see about that." Adam turned on his heel and stalked away.

His heart told him there was no way Emily could be interested in this arrogant little man. Her faith was too important to her. At the same time, his mind argued that they did have geographical background in common, if not philosophical beliefs. Mr. Wise was without doubt intelligent. Adam had met men like him in college. Intellectual giants with shriveled, stunted souls who denied the existence of God.

Emily was an intelligent, well-educated young woman. Surely, she recognized Wise for the empty shell he was. He watched the cocky little dandy through narrowed eyes. As soon as the opportunity presented itself, he would get her alone and warn her about Wise. Once she knew what sort of man he was, she would have no more to do with him. Then, with Wise out of the way, he would see Emily back to the Sloans' and begin a proper courtship. With that settled, Adam began to circulate and visit with his friends and neighbors.

❧

He was never able to talk to Emily alone. When she wasn't playing the piano, Charles Wise stayed at her side. Near the end of the evening, when it became apparent the young couples were preparing to leave, Adam approached them.

"I would like to speak to you in private, Miss Foster." He ignored the frowning man at her side. "May I see you home?"

Emily glanced at Michael and Sarah standing on her right, then turned her huge green eyes to Adam. "I came with Sarah and Michael—"

"Miss Foster came with me." Wise glared up at Adam. "Why don't you shove off, Jacobs? Find your own girl and leave mine alone."

At that moment, Adam would have liked nothing better than to punch Wise in the mouth. With a great deal of effort, he managed to bring his temper under control. Emily looked as miserable as he felt. She no more wanted to be with Wise than he wanted her to be.

"You are welcome to walk along with us, Adam," Michael offered with a smile.

Wise drew himself up to protest. "I don't think that is necessary."

"I'll grab my coat and be right with you."

The temperature was slightly below freezing, but with the warm sun shining down out of a cloudless sky and no breeze, it was a pleasant day for walking. Michael and Sarah stayed several paces ahead of the other three, who walked abreast with Emily between the two men. Copper trailed behind.

Emily vacillated between joy and embarrassment. Joy that Adam was at her side. Embarrassment that Charles Wise, on the other side, tried to hold her hand and acted as if he owned her. She eluded him for the second time by sticking both hands in her pockets.

"Do you enjoy teaching, Miss Foster?" Adam smiled down at her.

Her heart skipped a beat. "I do. I love it."

"Emily is the most talented teacher in the Sanctuary school." Charles took her elbow.

Emily! What must Adam be thinking of Mr. Wise's familiar use of her name, not to mention the proprietary manner in which he grasped her arm. "I suppose I am the best third- and fourth-grade teacher in Sanctuary." She managed a feeble laugh while attempting, without success, to extricate her arm. "But I'm certainly not the best teacher. Sarah is a wonderful teacher."

Her friends had advanced several paces ahead and were seemingly oblivious to her predicament. In a discreet attempt to jerk her arm away from Mr. Wise, she stumbled.

Immediately his arm went around her.

Enough was enough! "Mr. Wise, will you kindly remove your arm from my person?" She thought she heard Adam snicker. "Immediately!"

Charles's arm dropped away from her shoulders. His hand returned to her elbow. "Release me completely, sir. I am quite capable of walking alone."

"I was only being protective." Mr. Wise's voice contained a distinct whine that set Emily's teeth on edge. "It is a gentleman's duty to protect his lady."

"I am trying to be your friend." Emily scowled at the young man. "But I am certainly not your lady. If you misconstrued my actions, I am sorry." She took a deep breath. "I will continue to pray for you, Mr. Wise, but I do not wish to see you in a social situation ever again."

"Fine, if that is the way you feel, Miss Foster. I shall leave you to your uncouth cowboy and his smelly horse and I shall be on my way. When you see the error of your decision, let me know." He spun on his heel and headed back the way they had come.

Michael and Sarah had their heads together, and she could see their shoulders shaking. Adam whistled softly to himself. Emily had never seen anyone whistle and smile at the same time before. She ignored him and called ahead to her friend, "Sarah, don't you dare say you told me so."

Sarah and Michael slowed their pace so the other couple could catch up. "I did tell you so." Sarah smiled.

"You can't save someone who doesn't want to be saved, Emily," Michael said. "Only God can change Charles's heart."

"I know." Emily sighed. "It was foolish of me to ever get involved with a man like that."

"You weren't actually involved with him," Sarah soothed.

"I know, but obviously Mr. Wise thought I was interested

in him. I should have listened when you tried to warn me, Sarah."

Adam was still whistling. And smiling. Emily looked up at him. "Will you please stop that?"

"Yes, ma'am." Adam stopped whistling, but he continued to smile. Actually, it was more of a foolish grin. "I'm sorry, Miss Foster, but I'm only an uncouth cowboy. I didn't know any better."

They all laughed. Then Michael said, "We do need to make Charles a subject of prayer, don't you agree?"

Both young women agreed readily. Adam took a minute to think about it before nodding in affirmation. That settled, the four walked along together with Copper trailing behind. The conversation soon turned to school and the need for a more comprehensive library.

"I thought we might have some sort of fund-raiser," Emily ventured.

"Sounds like a good idea," Michael agreed. "Do you girls have any thoughts on what we could do to raise money?"

"Maybe a pie supper," Sarah suggested. "Or a box social."

"I don't believe I have ever heard of either," Emily said. "How do they work?"

"You girls cook good things to eat," Adam said.

"And we men eat everything." Michael finished his sentence.

"That sounds like fun," Emily remarked. "At least for the men."

"I can attest to the fact that Miss Foster makes a raisin pie that can't be beat," Adam said.

"I'm sure Emily is a wonderful cook." Michael smiled. "But you'd have to go a long way to top Sarah's dried apple pie."

"That is very flattering." Emily blushed. "But I was asking about the procedure."

"The women cook a meal and put it in a box they decorate,"

Adam explained. "The boxes are auctioned off to the men, and the highest bidder has the pleasure of sharing it with the lady who did the cooking."

"A pie supper works the same way," Michael added.

"Except you only need to bake a pie instead of a whole meal," Sarah clarified. "They are both a lot of fun."

They spent the remainder of the short walk brainstorming ideas to raise money before finally agreeing on a box social to be held sometime in the spring.

"In the meantime, we could ask for donations," Emily suggested.

"Of money or books?" Sarah asked.

"Either would be nice," Emily said. "What do you think, Mr. Jacobs?"

"I'm the only one here who isn't a teacher," Adam replied. "But since you asked—why not both?"

As they neared the Sloans' house, Michael and Sarah walked on ahead. Emily smiled when she noticed they were holding hands. Adam evidently noticed, too.

"What would happen if I asked to hold your hand, Miss Foster?" he asked.

Emily slanted a saucy smile at him. "I suppose you will never know unless you ask, Mr. Jacobs."

Adam grinned. "Miss Foster, may I hold your hand?"

She slipped her small hand into his. "You may."

Though they both wore gloves, she felt the warmth of his hand all the way up her arm.

"Miss Foster?"

"Yes, Mr. Jacobs?"

"May I call you Emily?"

"You may."

"Emily?" Her name fell sweetly from his lips.

"Yes, Mr. Jacobs?"

"I recollect I asked you to call me Adam. And if memory serves, you agreed."

"I believe you are correct, Adam."

"May I escort you to church Sunday morning?"

"May Sarah come along?"

"She may."

"Then I shall look forward to Sunday morning."

As soon as Sarah closed the door, the two girls burst into giggles. When they could finally talk, Emily said, "I saw Brother Michael holding your hand."

"Emily, for the first time, he talked to me as an equal, not as Ben's little sister." Sarah hugged herself. "Come out to the kitchen and tell me what Adam said. And don't leave out a single word."

"You are such a busybody, Sarah."

"I know." Sarah began to laugh again, and Emily joined in.

fourteen

Sunday morning dawned sunny and cold. Emily surveyed her meager wardrobe, finally selecting a new cranberry red woolen dress that complimented her black hair and ivory skin.

As she put the finishing touches on her hair, there was a gentle tap on the door and Sarah poked her head in. "Good. You are ready." Then she covered her mouth to suppress a giggle. "Oh, Emily, you look lovely."

"Is my hair all right?" Emily ran her hand over her upswept hairdo. "I thought I would try something a bit different."

"It's perfect. I like the curls framing your face." Sarah stepped into the room and circled Emily, studying her carefully as she moved around her. "You are always perfectly groomed, but there is something different about you today." She tilted her head to one side. "I'll put my finger on the change in a minute."

Emily watched Sarah's reflection in the mirror. Obviously, her friend was teasing, but she didn't mind.

"I know what it is." Sarah snapped her fingers. "It's your eyes."

"My eyes?"

"Yes, that's definitely it. They are all soft and dreamy looking. You know, like someone who's—oh, I don't know." Sarah giggled. "Maybe in love."

Emily frowned. "Would that be anything like the expression in your own eyes?"

"Maybe."

Both girls smiled. Then Emily picked up her Bible and

swept from the room, saying over her shoulder, "Come along, Miss Sloan. And try to conduct yourself with at least a semblance of dignity. After all, you are supposed to be my chaperone."

The two young women were standing in the parlor window, concealed by the lace curtains, when Adam rode up on Copper. They quickly backed away from the window.

"Do I really look all right, Sarah?" Emily ran a hand over her hair, then touched the scrap of lace at her throat. "Is my collar straight?"

"You are perfect, Emily."

"Do you think I should go to the door?"

"I would wait until he knocks." Sarah grinned. "You don't want to appear too eager."

"Of course not. I meant when he knocks." Emily smoothed her skirt. "Maybe I should have worn the green dress."

"Your dress is perfect. Now quit worrying."

"I wonder what is taking him so long. Maybe he changed his mind. Maybe—" She moved to the window and peered through the lace curtains. "Oh, my!" She turned to Sarah with wide eyes. "Adam isn't alone."

"What do you mean?" Sarah lifted the edge of the curtain and peeked out. "Oh!" She dropped the curtain and stepped back. "That's Michael with him."

"Yes, I know."

Sarah's hands flew to her hair. "I should have taken more pains with my hair, and this dress—I should have worn something more mature. I look like a child in this dress. Why didn't he tell me he was coming?"

"Goodness, Sarah, Brother Michael has known you forever. You don't have to impress him."

"Yes, I do. I used to wear Ben's old overalls."

"What has that to do with anything? You were going to

wear that dress to church. He would have seen you in it anyway."

"But that would have been different. Escorting me to church, well, that's like he has come calling."

"He has come calling, and you are beautiful, as always." Emily picked up her Bible as a knock sounded at the door. "Now I believe that is the second time they have knocked. Which of us shall answer the door?"

⋙

Sometime later, Emily relaxed against the back of the buggy seat. It was a perfect day for a Sunday afternoon buggy ride. It had been a perfect day, period. She drank in her surroundings. She loved the snowcapped mountains, the open land that seemed to stretch on forever, and the sky. Especially the sky. *How Papa would have loved it here.* Emily sighed.

"That was quite a sigh. Was it a good sigh or a not-so-good one?"

She turned toward Adam. His smile was so tender, it brought tears to her eyes.

"I was thinking how my father would have enjoyed being here. He always talked about the mountains and the sky. Especially the sky. He said the sky stretched on forever, blue and unsullied by factory smoke."

"I should imagine it is very different from New York City or Chicago." *Gertrude was born and raised in Chicago. She hated Montana.* "I suppose some people would find it boring."

"Oh, no!" Emily protested. "It isn't boring. It's beautiful and majestic and serene. New York was crowded and dirty and dangerous."

"There is danger here, too." Adam squeezed her hand. "My father was killed by an angry bull."

"I'm so sorry, Adam. I knew he died in some sort of accident, but I didn't know exactly how."

"It shouldn't have happened. Dad was always so careful, but this one time he turned his back at the wrong time." His hand tightened on Emily's hand. "I think I told you I was studying to be a doctor, but I'd only been in college a couple of months when Dad was killed. I had to give all that up and come home. John and my mother needed me."

The sympathy in Emily's wide green eyes spurred him on to a confession that shamed him. "I was angry at my father for being careless, and I was angry at God for taking my dad and destroying all my plans."

"Oh, Adam, I'm so sorry." Tears welled up and rolled down Emily's cheeks.

Adam pulled off his glove and brushed them away with his thumb. Her skin felt soft as velvet. "Don't be sorry. I'm not. I *am* sorry about my dad," he clarified his thought, "and I'm sorry about my rebellion, but I'm not sorry about my plans. Those were my plans, not God's. I never once asked Him what He wanted me to do with my life."

"There was nothing wrong with you wanting to be a physician."

"It wasn't wrong in and of itself, but I think my motives were wrong." His expression grew serious. "I have thought about this a lot lately. I've tried to remember why I wanted to be a physician."

"I should imagine you wanted to help people."

Adam's laugh was short and bitter. "I don't believe my motives were so noble. My pride told me I would become the best doctor in the West. I wanted fame and recognition. Or at least I thought I did. My life was in ashes when you came to Sanctuary, Emily. I might as well admit, I was less than thrilled when the Thompson brothers told me they had sent for a mail-order bride."

"Really?" A dimple played around the corner of Emily's

mouth. "You did a wonderful job of hiding your displeasure."

Adam allowed himself a small answering smile before his face once more grew serious. "I'm ashamed of the way I treated you that day at the depot. Please forgive me."

"Of course I forgive you. And if it makes you feel any better, remember I never planned on marrying you. You were merely my way out of an untenable situation."

"Ouch!" Adam winced. "It must be a day for confessions."

"So it would seem." Emily turned her head to the distant mountains. When she looked at Adam again, her eyes were serious. "Tell me about Sarah's cousin Gertrude."

Adam didn't say anything for several heartbeats. Then he took a deep breath. "Trudy was one of those strange women King Solomon warned foolish young men about in Proverbs. She was beautiful, or at least I thought so at the time. I was infatuated with her from the moment I met her, and before I knew what had happened, we were engaged to be married." He rubbed the back of his neck. "To be perfectly honest, I'm not sure who did the proposing. But anyway, for about two weeks, I was head over heels in love with her; then I knew I didn't want to spend the rest of my life with her. One night, she took off, and I was saved the trouble of breaking the engagement."

"I overheard John say you mourned Gertrude for a year." Emily's green eyes searched his face, demanding the truth.

"I suppose in a way that's true." The color rose in Adam's face. "It's a funny thing about human nature—at least the male of the species. Women may view things different. I was pretty much over whatever it was I felt for Trudy by the time she left, but the thought that she would abandon me hurt my pride. I guess everybody took wounded vanity to be a broken heart, and I let them think what they liked. I even tried to convince myself that I loved her. If you believe a lie long enough, it becomes the truth. In my mind, I built Trudy up until she became the most beautiful woman who ever lived." His eyes met Emily's. "I was angry at my dad and God and almost everyone else. Remember, I wasn't a very pleasant person when you first met me. Then something happened that changed everything. It was as though blinders were removed from my eyes, and I saw clearly for the first time in years."

Emily remembered Sarah saying that Adam's pride had been hurt more than his heart when Gertrude left. His eyes begged her to believe him, and she wanted to. More than anything, she wanted to believe he had never really loved Gertrude.

Father, help me to know the truth. Emily's short prayer was answered immediately by another memory.

"I believe you," she said.

"You do?" His words rushed out as if he had been holding his breath. "I mean, I was telling the truth, but I wasn't sure you would—I mean, why should you trust me?"

"Because I was there."

"You were where?"

"It was after I had been so sick. I was feeling better and I came outside one morning. Don't you remember?" She blushed at the memory of interrupting what had been a private moment between Adam and his heavenly Father. "You were there. I saw you raise your hands to heaven and shout, 'Thank You, Lord.' I knew that morning you had made peace with God."

"Was it that obvious?"

"Yes." She smiled. "That morning was when I first knew that I could come to love—" Color flooded her face. "I mean, like you. I knew that morning we could be friends."

"I was hoping we could be more than friends. Do you think that's possible, Emily?"

"Maybe." She tried to look away, but his dark eyes held her captive.

"May I kiss you, Emily?"

"I'm not sure that would be proper, Adam."

"We are friends."

"Yes. Yes, we are."

"Maybe we're a little more than friends."

"Maybe."

"We might become much more than friends."

"The contract I signed gave us six months to make a decision about that."

"Oh, yes. The escape clause." Adam smiled. "I believe the Thompson brothers did mention that."

"You know I didn't like you much when I first met you?"

"Yes, I know that." He leaned closer. His warm breath caressed her face. "I wasn't overly fond of you, either."

I should say no. I should—I really should say no. She fought a losing battle with her decorum. "You may kiss me, Adam."

Other than her hand clasped in his, he didn't touch her but merely leaned closer until their lips met. Emily's world spun in that brief moment of contact. When he drew away, she opened her eyes and looked at him. What she saw in his eyes confirmed what she sensed in her own heart. A covenant had been sealed between the two of them.

Adam cleared his throat. "You must be cold."

For the first time, she noticed she was, indeed, cold. "Yes, I am."

He reached over the back of the buggy seat and pulled out a plaid blanket. He draped the blanket across her lap and, with the utmost tenderness, gently tucked it around her. It had been so long since anyone treated her with such care. Her breath caught in her throat. She blinked back tears.

"Thank you," she whispered.

"You are welcome." He put his arm around her and urged her closer to him, then he picked up the lines, and the buggy once more began to roll.

"It's so beautiful here." Emily snuggled against the warmth of his arm. "Have you always lived in Montana?"

"I was born in Missouri." Adam looked out across the vast prairie to the snowcapped mountains. "My parents came here as homesteaders when I was four years old. It took five years for them to prove up on their six hundred and forty acres. Dad was able to buy more land as time went by. When John reached twenty-one years, he homesteaded his own section, then we bought a few more acres, until we now have over two thousand acres."

That sounded like a lot of land to Emily, but she knew, in what had been termed the Great American Desert, it wasn't. Her father had told her it took as much as ten acres to graze one cow. For a brief moment, she allowed herself to feel sad that Papa hadn't lived to see this majestic land, then she reminded herself that Mama and Papa were in a land that was beautiful beyond anything she could imagine.

"You didn't homestead because of college."

"That's right." He smiled at her. "John hadn't proved up on his claim when my dad died, and my mom needed me."

"So you stayed with your mother?"

"I did until John proved up on his claim; then he married Ruth, and they moved in with Mom. After that, I built the cabin where I live now. The following winter there was a flu epidemic. Mom and Ruth were both sick. Mom died. Ruth recovered, but she lost the child she was carrying."

"How sad for all of you."

He looked at her. "That's the way life is, I guess. You've experienced losses."

"Yes," Emily agreed. She didn't want to talk about her own

life at the moment, so she asked, "Weren't sheep raised here?"

"At one time, but they are gone now."

"Yes, I read about the range wars."

"This is John's homestead." Adam pointed to a small sod building. "That's the soddy where John lived for five years while he proved up his land."

Emily studied the tiny building. There was only one small window. The plank door hung by a single leather hinge. "It looks lonely and depressing."

"That's why John and Ruth weren't married until after he had proved up on his claim. He didn't want her to have to live out here and fight the snakes and bugs."

Emily thought about Ruth's immaculate house. She would never have been able to cope with the dirt sifting down on everything.

"Much as I hate to do it"—Adam's words broke in on her thoughts—"I think it's time I took you back to town."

The sun hung low in the western sky, giving the scattering of puffy clouds a rosy touch. "Yes, I suppose it is about time to go home."

"The Thompsons live about a mile down the road. Since they're on the way back to town, why don't we stop and visit them for a few minutes?"

Emily sensed that he was as reluctant to see this day end as she was. "I think I would enjoy visiting the Thompson family."

"You'll like them." Adam visibly relaxed. "John and I grew up with Ike and Lewis. Lewis is my best friend."

"Oh, really?" Emily couldn't resist teasing. "Isn't Lewis the one who decided to buy you a mail-order bride?"

"I wouldn't exactly say he bought you."

"It seemed that way to me." She shot him a mischievous look. "I thought there must be something terribly wrong with a man who had to resort to buying a wife."

"And I thought a woman who would allow herself to be bought must be desperate for a husband." He put his arm around her and drew her close. "I guess I was mistaken about that."

She leaned against his solid warmth. "I was mistaken, too. There is nothing wrong with you, Adam." She sighed. "But I was desperate. Not for a husband but for escape."

"And so you escaped to Sanctuary?"

"Yes, I did."

His arm tightened before he released her. "I'm glad that you did."

"So am I."

fifteen

Emily had met the Thompsons briefly at church, but this was her first opportunity to visit with Bertha and Kirsten. The two women were as different as night and day. Bertha was a tall, thin, sharp-featured woman with piercing black eyes and dark hair who rarely smiled. Kirsten was a short, blond, blue-eyed dumpling of a girl with a sweet smile that never left her pretty, dimpled face.

Adam and the tall, gangly Thompson brothers, who reminded Emily of portraits she had seen of Abraham Lincoln, gathered around the kitchen table with steaming cups of coffee and massive pieces of apple pie. Their main topic of conversation, as far as Emily could tell, was cattle prices. She gladly followed the sisters-in-law into the parlor.

As soon as the women were seated in the chilly room with its stiff Victorian furnishings, Kirsten began to ask Emily questions.

"Do you like Montana?"

"Very much." Emily smiled.

"It's different, though, isn't it?" Kirsten giggled. "I mean, it's certainly different from the dairy farm where I grew up."

"I was raised in New York City." Emily shifted a bit, trying to find a comfortable spot in the padded chair. "But it was always my father's dream to come west. I came to share that dream."

"Did you work in a factory?" Kirsten leaned forward. "When my uncle decided it was time for me to earn my own way, that was what I thought I would have to do. Then I read Lewis's advertisement in a magazine, and here I am." She giggled. "Is that what happened to you? Did you read Mr. Jacobs's letter in a magazine?"

"Not exactly." Emily took a sip of coffee and glanced around the austere room. It certainly was dreary.

"We are going to build our own house in the spring," Kirsten announced. "With the baby coming and all—"

"Kirsten, I don't think Miss Foster is interested in your personal affairs." Though Bertha couldn't have been more than in her midtwenties, she looked as rigid and unyielding as the chair Emily sat in. She turned the conversation from Kirsten. "Do you enjoy teaching, Miss Foster?"

"Yes, I do." Emily's smile fell on the stone wall of Bertha's countenance. "My father was a teacher. If Mama's health hadn't failed, I would have taught sooner."

"I told Ike and Lewis it was a fool idea writing that letter." She sniffed. "They had no call to go interfering in your life."

"But she likes Montana, don't you, Emily?" Kirsten asked.

Emily smiled at the bubbly blond girl. "I love Montana. It is everything I dreamed of and more."

"See, Bertha." Kirsten giggled. "Everything works to the good of God's children. Don't you think so, Emily?"

"Yes, as a matter of fact, I do."

"I never said I didn't believe things work out as they are intended to," Bertha said. "I just happen to believe we shouldn't interfere in the Lord's work."

Emily decided it was time to ask some questions of her own. "Where were you born, Bertha?"

"A couple of miles down the road." She drew herself up. "My kinfolk were pioneers."

Emily thought how nice it must be for Bertha to have her family so close. She wondered what Bertha's parents were like and was on the verge of asking when Bertha volunteered. "Pa always had the wanderlust. Right after me and Ike was married five years ago, he decided he wanted to see Oregon."

"It must have been hard on your mother. I mean, leaving you behind."

"I wouldn't think so." Bertha sniffed. "Ma was a true pioneer woman. She went where her man said they would go. She didn't fuss none, neither." She stood up abruptly and left the room.

Emily looked at Kirsten. The plump blond giggled. "Don't mind Bertha. She isn't nearly as bad as she seems."

"I hope I didn't offend her."

"You didn't." Kirsten picked up her coffee cup. "She heard Tad stirring around and went to see about him. It's cold in here. Let's go back to the kitchen."

Emily followed Kirsten to the warm kitchen. Several minutes later, after she and Adam left the Thompson family home, they discovered that the sun now hung low on the horizon and the temperature had dropped.

"I should imagine we'll have snow by the end of the week," Adam said.

"Do you think we'll have another blizzard?"

"What do you mean another blizzard?" Adam grinned down at her. "That was just a skiff we had earlier."

Emily thought of the blinding snowstorm shortly after her arrival. Surely, Adam was teasing. She smiled at him and didn't respond.

"What did you think of the Thompsons?" He changed the subject.

"Bertha is a bit reserved."

"Bertie prides herself on being a stoic pioneer, but she has a good heart."

"Kirsten said she was raised on a dairy farm in upper New York State."

"Lewis told me her mother died when she was born. Her

mother's sister and her husband raised her. When she was six-teen, her uncle told her it was time she made her own way."

"So she married Lewis Thompson." Emily recalled the way Lewis had kept grinning at her and punching Adam's arm when they were leaving. She would rather have worked at the Triangle Shirtwaist Company until she died of old age than to have married Lewis Thompson.

"We should spend more time with Lewis and his wife. I know you and Kirsten have a lot in common, and Lewis is like a brother to me."

Emily sighed. Adam put his arm around her and pulled her close. She rested her head against his shoulder. Despite the biting cold and the fact that her nose felt like it was fro-zen, a cozy warmth crept over her. Bertha's words echoed in her mind. *"A pioneer woman goes where her man says, and she don't fuss none, neither."*

"We will have to visit the Thompsons often," she mur-mured and received a quick grin and nod from Adam.

❧

"I want to know everything that happened," Sarah demanded. The two young women were alone in Molly Sloan's warm kitchen sharing a pot of hot tea before they went to bed. "And I do mean everything."

"Sarah, you are such a snoop."

"We both know that." Sarah giggled. "Now tell me." She shook a scolding finger at Emily. "Don't you dare leave out even one juicy morsel."

"Let me see." Emily took a delicate sip of tea. "I sat beside Adam in church when I wasn't playing the piano."

"I know that." Sarah squirmed in her chair. "I mean later. You know, after Ruth invited you to Sunday dinner. Oh, that reminds me. You will never guess who sneaked into church late and left just before dismissal." Not waiting for Emily's guess, she rushed on. "Charles Wise, that's who. Michael had just stepped behind the pulpit and he saw him. What do you make of that?"

"I don't know." Emily shrugged. "Maybe Mr. Wise is seeking the truth."

"That's what Michael thinks. He says we should pray for Mr. Wise." She waved a hand, dismissing him from the conversation. "Now tell me everything."

"We had a wonderful dinner. Ruth is a marvelous cook, and I fear I ate too much. The custard pie was absolutely wonderful. I could have eaten the whole thing by myself." She lifted the teacup to her lips and took a leisurely drink while Sarah fidgeted in her chair.

"I don't want to know what was on the menu. I want to know what you and Adam did. Tell me!"

Emily shook her head. "I don't know what I'm going to do with you, Sarah."

"You know you love me." Sarah giggled. "Now tell me!"

Emily sighed. "After dinner, I helped Ruth clean up the kitchen. Then Adam suggested we go for a buggy ride before he brought me home. So we did."

Emily stood and carried her cup and saucer to the sink. "Now I think I shall call it a day."

"That's all? Surely you talked about something."

"We surely did." Emily smiled at her friend. "But what we talked about is personal. Not even my dearest friend in the whole world needs to know everything about my life. Some things are too precious to share."

"I guess," Sarah agreed. "So he brought you straight home?"

"We visited the Thompsons." Emily poured a small amount of water in the dishpan and washed her cup. "I met them briefly at church, but this was my first chance to get acquainted with Bertha and Kirsten."

Sarah joined her at the sink. "How did you like them?"

"They are all right." Emily dried her cup. "I don't know how they live in the same house. Bertha is so stern, and Kirsten is so. . .oh, I don't know. . .young."

"*Silly* is the word I would have used." Sarah put their cups in the cupboard. "Privately I call them The Pioneer Woman and The Milkmaid."

"Sarah! That isn't very polite." Emily dried her hands on the dish towel. She held her laughter in check.

"I know, but it is appropriate. How did you like Lewis?"

"Lewis Thompson? I'm sure he's a very nice man."

"Um-hum." Sarah nodded. "He's Adam's best friend. Though to be perfectly honest, I could never understand why."

"Adam wants us to spend more time with Kirsten and Lewis. So I suppose we will." She hung up the dish towel. "Bertha would say since he's Adam's friend, I shouldn't ask questions. A pioneer woman does what her man says."

"And she don't fuss none, neither," Sarah added with a mischievous grin.

"I see you've talked to Bertha." Emily bent to put out the lamp.

"Oh, yes." Sarah giggled. "I've known Bertha forever. But I'm not nearly as well acquainted with her as you are going to be by the end of this winter."

Emily couldn't stifle a slight groan.

Sarah laughed. "You can spend some of your courting evenings with Michael and me."

"With you and Michael?" Emily questioned. "I think it's your turn to talk about what happened while I was gone."

"Oh, Emily." Sarah grasped Emily's arm. "Michael came to dinner today, and afterward he had a long talk with Father." She squeezed Emily's arm. "Michael asked Father's permission to come calling."

"On your father?" Emily couldn't resist teasing.

"No, silly, on my father's daughter. Me."

Emily felt a momentary flash of envy that her father wasn't here to give Adam permission to call on her. Then she put her feelings aside and hugged Sarah. "I'm so happy for you."

"I guess it's a bit old-fashioned. I mean, asking Daddy's permission. But Michael is a courtly, proper sort of man. That's one reason I love him so much." Her sigh was deep and dreamy. "Maybe we can have a double wedding, Emily."

"In my case, I think you are getting a bit ahead of yourself, Sarah. Adam hasn't even mentioned love."

"He will," Sarah predicted. "I know he will."

"Maybe," Emily agreed and hoped with all her heart that Sarah was right.

&

"I love her, John." Adam paced back and forth in Ruth's kitchen. "I want to marry Emily."

"You've only known her a couple of months." John squinted at his younger brother over the rim of his coffee cup. "Don't you think you might be rushing things a bit?"

"No." Adam dropped in a chair across from his brother. "Remember how Dad called Mom a Proverbs 31 woman, John? Emily is like Mom. I can trust her. She's strong in her faith and she's honorable. She is the sort of woman a man feels proud to have walking beside him." He ran his fingers through his hair. "She's beautiful and smart and good and kind."

"I remember not too long ago you described Emily as scrawny and desperate for a husband."

"If I said that, I shouldn't have." The color rose in Adam's face. "I was angry at Lewis for butting into my business. It didn't have anything to do with Emily."

"Adam, Ruth has been praying for this almost from the day Emily arrived, and I'd be proud to have Emily join our family." John set his cup down on the table. "Just take it easy and don't rush things."

"Faint heart never won fair lady." Adam laughed. "We still have four months to make a decision. I decided today we should honor that contract."

John nodded. "I think that's a good idea. It will give you time to really get to know one another." He pushed back his chair and stood. "Well, little brother, I think it's time for bed."

"I guess it is getting late." Adam stood and extended a hand to his brother. "Thanks, John."

The brothers clasped hands, then John clapped his free hand on Adam's shoulder. "I don't say it nearly enough, Adam, but I'm proud of you. I'm honored to have you as my brother."

"I love you, too, John. I don't know what I would do without you." He slapped John on the shoulder, then shrugged into his heavy sheepskin-lined coat.

Large snowflakes swirled slowly through the frigid air when Adam stepped outside. He had built up a good fire before he went to John and Ruth's, and he'd only been gone a half hour at most. Still, when he opened his door and stepped inside, the coldness of the empty house hit him in the face. He shivered. He had lived alone for a number of years, but he didn't remember ever feeling so lonely.

"And the LORD God said, It is not good that the man should be alone." The words from Genesis echoed in his mind as clearly as if they had been spoken aloud. "Man wasn't meant to be alone." His words sounded loud in the silence. "God willing, this is the last winter I'll spend here by myself. In the next four months, I intend to spend every moment I can spare with Emily."

He went to bed thinking he should surely be able to see her three or four evenings a week, plus all day Sunday. He fell asleep trying to decide which evenings would be best for her.

sixteen

Shortly after midnight, Adam woke with a start. For a heart-beat, he couldn't think what had roused him. Then he knew.

"Blizzard," he mumbled as he rolled from the warmth of his bed and pulled on his clothes. His small house creaked and popped, then trembled in the fury of the wind. He lit a lantern and stuffed a couple of changes of clothes and his razor into a canvas carryall. At his front door, he hesitated before extinguishing the light. The lantern would be next to useless in what awaited him on the other side of the closed door. He set the lantern inside the door. Taking a deep breath, he wound a woolen muffler around the lower part of his face; then, shouldering the carryall, he opened the door and stepped outside.

Stinging snow cut into his eyes and the exposed skin of his forehead. He pulled the muffler up over his eyes, grasped the rope secured beside his front door, and stepped into the maelstrom. The wind buffeted him. He stumbled then fell to his knees. He struggled to his feet. Clinging to the rope that was now his lifeline, he forced himself on. His hands had gone numb. Thinking he might have lost the rope, he felt a moment of panic.

Father, help me! The words of entreaty were barely uttered through the silence of his mind when he felt peace. The rope was still in his hand. His fingers were so cold inside the heavy glove, he couldn't feel it. He felt he had been in the storm for hours when he stumbled against something solid. Once more, he dropped to his knees. Then, reaching up with his free hand, he pulled the muffler down from his eyes and staggered up the steps and across John's back porch.

A rectangle of light appeared before him. He dropped the rope and allowed his brother to pull him into the warmth of the kitchen. John unwound the frozen muffler, while Ruth pulled off his gloves and massaged his hands. John took the carryall from his shoulder, then helped him out of his coat.

"I'm all right." His teeth chattered so violently, it was an effort to get out the words. They led him to a chair in front of the open oven door. As soon as he collapsed in the chair, John pulled off his boots and socks.

"I don't see any sign of frostbite," he said.

Ruth pressed a mug of hot coffee in his hands.

When he grew warm enough to speak, he said, "I shouldn't have built my house so far from yours."

"As I recall, when you built the house, you wanted it even farther away." John poured a cup of coffee and sat down beside his brother. "At the time you wanted to be a hermit."

"Yeah." Adam managed a sheepish grin. "Well, I was an idiot."

"A mite confused perhaps." John chuckled. "But you were young."

"I was ripe pickin's for Trudy Phillips." Adam heaved a sigh. "You know, it's funny, John, as angry as I was with God, He was still watching over me."

"You belonged to Him, Adam. No man—or woman—can pluck you out of God's hand."

"I'm thankful He prevented me from becoming more involved with her." He took a swallow of coffee. "Because she was willing, John." The color rose in his face. "If you understand what I mean."

"I understand." John stood. "We were praying for you, little brother."

"I know you were." Adam took his cup to the sink.

John joined his brother. "What would you have done had she stayed?"

"I've asked myself that same question."

"And?"

"I'd probably have married her because it would have been the honorable thing to do." Adam shook his head. "And I would have been miserable for the rest of my life. I'm thankful that things turned out as they did."

"Me, too." John clapped a hand on the younger man's shoulder. "Now shall we go out and stir up the cattle?"

Adam groaned. "I guess we'd better."

ea.

When Emily went to bed, moonlight streamed through the window. When she woke shortly after midnight, the room looked as dark as the inside of a closet. The wind moaned a deep, rushing undertone to the shrill, whistling notes that shrieked against the window. She felt the battering of the wind against the house. The windowpanes rattled, and the house trembled against the onslaught. She remembered the last blizzard and knew that Adam and John would be out in the storm keeping the cattle awake and moving.

Father, keep them safe. Keep all the men who are out in this storm safe.

A heavy comforter lay folded at the foot of the bed. She reached down and pulled it over her, then snuggled into the added warmth. Unable to sleep, she allowed her thoughts to wander.

She thought of her afternoon at the Jacobses' place. She had enjoyed the time she spent with Ruth. Ruth and John's baby would be born in five months. While they worked together in the kitchen after dinner, Ruth had confided in her that she was beginning to feel movement. Her first baby, she said, was lost before she ever felt quickening. When she talked about the coming child, her face glowed.

Emily wondered how long it would be before she saw Ruth again. She snuggled deeper under the weight of the covers as her thoughts turned to Adam. She remembered the first time she saw him. She had thought he was the most arrogant man she had ever met. When he refused to take her to a boardinghouse but brought her instead to Ruth, she had been angry. Or as angry as her illness allowed her to be. In retrospect and viewed through the eyes of love, she recognized his imperious manner as compassion. If not for Ruth's gentle ministrations, she might have died.

The house creaked and shuddered in the violence of the storm. Frozen pellets hammered against the window. Emily pulled the covers over her ears in a vain attempt to muffle the sound of the storm.

Light filled the room, and she turned to see the shadowed form of Molly Sloan standing in the doorway holding a lamp. "Are you all right, dear?"

Emily peeked out from the covers. "I'm fine. Thank you."

"Are you warm enough?"

"Yes."

"Then I will see you in the morning."

As she turned to leave, Emily blinked back tears. "Thank you, Mrs. Sloan."

The room grew a shade brighter as the woman turned back. "Whatever for, dear?"

"For caring about me," Emily said. "You remind me of my mother."

"In some respects, all mothers are the same." Mrs. Sloan's laugh was soft in the dimness of the room. "It's our nature to see to our family. Good night, Emily."

"Good night, Mrs. Sloan."

The light moved away, then disappeared.

Mrs. Sloan's kindness brought memories of Emily's own mother to her. Tears overflowed, and she turned her face into the pillow to blot them. Mama had been her best friend. How she longed to tell her about Adam and about all the things that had happened to her since Mama and Papa went away.

She whispered just as if her mother were there. "Remember how we prayed for the man I would someday marry, Mama? We asked that he be honorable and kind and faithful. And most of all, we asked that he know and serve the Lord." She sniffled. "Well, although I couldn't see it at first, I think God answered all our prayers when he brought Adam into my life. He is all of those things and so much more. He hasn't asked me to marry him yet. But I think he soon will. I love him, Mama. I want more than anything to be his wife. I wish you and Papa could meet him. I know you would approve."

Emily fell asleep and dreamed that her mother sat beside her on the bed. Mama held her hand between hers, and they laughed together. The lamplight cast a soft glow on the room, and she realized Mama wasn't blind anymore.

When Emily woke the next morning, she saw the lacy white pattern of frost on the window beside her bed. The storm still raged outside. She threw the warm covers back and stepped on the cold floor so she could reach the window. With her fingernail, she scraped a small peek hole in the frost. Outside she could see nothing but snow blowing and swirling a solid sheet of white.

Wednesday afternoon, the blizzard ended. The wind died down, and in the clear blue sky, the sun shone brightly. Thursday morning, Emily and Sarah returned to school. The wind had swept the earth clean in some spots. In others, the snow drifted as high as the top of Emily's head. That afternoon when school dismissed, Emily left the building with Sarah and Michael. Though she knew the roads were impassable, she looked for Adam. Even knowing he would not be there did not stop her keen disappointment. He wasn't waiting in front of the school on Friday night, either.

Only the farmers and ranchers who lived within a short distance of town were in church on Sunday morning. Emily again felt a sharp stab of disappointment when the Jacobs family wasn't numbered among them.

Monday afternoon when Emily walked through the schoolhouse door with Michael and Sarah, she saw Adam. Her heart leaped with joy when he swung down from the wagon seat and came to meet them.

"I thought you might like a ride home." His smile lit his face.

"We sure would," Michael said. Sarah dug an elbow into his ribs and shook her head. "But I guess we can't."

"Michael and I are stopping at the mercantile," Sarah added. "Remember, Michael?"

"Oh, yeah." His eyes twinkled as he snapped his fingers. "How could I have forgotten?"

"I guess you and Emily will have to go without us." Sarah smiled. "I hope you don't mind, Emily."

"No, that's fine." She could have hugged her friends, especially since it was obvious Michael and Sarah had made up an excuse to leave her alone with Adam. She decided to test Adam. "Are you sure I don't need to go, too?"

"I'm sure they can take care of things on their own." Adam took Emily's arm and hustled her over to the wagon.

Michael and Sarah waved and walked away with their heads together. Adam helped Emily up onto the high wagon seat. He hurried and climbed onto the driver's seat and picked up the reins.

"I had to come into town for supplies," he said, indicating the canvas-covered bundles in the back of the wagon. "I thought, since I was in town anyway, I would come by and see how you made it through the storm."

Emily felt a stab of disappointment. Had she merely been an afterthought? "We did quite well, thank you. School reopened on Thursday."

"I suppose attendance was down at church Sunday."

"Most of the townspeople were there, as well as the farmers and ranchers who live nearby." She glanced at him from the corner of her eye. "Brother Michael saw Charles Wise slip in late and leave early, the same as he did last Sunday."

He didn't say anything, but Emily saw his jaw tighten. "We couldn't get out before today."

"I remember last time." Emily turned her gaze to the road in front of them. "I knew the roads would be impassable."

Adam glanced at her. She sat primly with her hands folded in her lap. He thought they had reached an understanding on Sunday, but she didn't seem very friendly today. Was she angry with him? Had he done or said something to offend her? Or had he misinterpreted the kiss they shared? To him it had been a promise sealed. He thought it had been the same for her.

He pulled the horses to the side of the road. They might as well get this settled right now. "Emily, I would like a word with you."

She turned to face him, her green eyes questioning.

He wrapped the lines around the brake handle. "Are you angry at me?"

"No, of course not." Her lower lip trembled, and her eyes appeared suspiciously bright.

"If I have done anything to offend you, I wish you would tell me what it is." He took her hand in his. She tried to pull away, but he refused to relinquish his hold. "I thought we had an understanding."

Two big tears rolled down her cheeks, breaking his heart. "Come on, sweetheart. If you cry, your face will freeze."

"I worried about you all week." She dabbed at the tears with a mitten-clad hand. "Every time I thought of you out in the blizzard trying to keep those stupid cows moving, I prayed for you." She turned her head away. "You never even thought about me."

"Never thought about you?" Adam chuckled, then he laughed. "You are all I thought about."

She turned to search his face. "Really?"

"Really. John had to practically hog-tie me to keep me from coming into town on Wednesday." He put his arm around her and drew her close.

She offered no resistance and snuggled against him. "The roads would have been too bad on Wednesday."

"They weren't any too good today. I had to shovel several places so the horse could get through with the wagon."

"But Ruth had to have supplies."

"Ruth has enough food stocked up to get a dozen people through the winter."

Emily thought of Ruth's pantry with the gleaming jars of fruits and vegetables and the equally well-stocked cellar. "If Ruth didn't need anything, wouldn't it have been easier to get out on horseback?"

"It would have." His arm tightened around her. "But I couldn't very well have seen you home on horseback."

He had come all the way to town through the aftermath of a blizzard just to see her. Her heart sang with joy.

His arm dropped away from her shoulders, and he took both her hands in his. "I love you with all my heart." She saw the reflection of her face in the depths of his brown eyes. "I want to spend the rest of my life with you." His hands tightened on hers. "If you will do me the honor of becoming my wife, I promise I will love and cherish you forever. Emily, will you marry me?"

She thought this must surely be the happiest day of her life. To her utter astonishment, she burst into tears. Clinging to the lapels of Adam's rough coat, she buried her face against his chest and sobbed.

Adam held her close and patted her back until the tears were all used up. When she pulled away, she saw the concern on his face through tear-dimmed eyes.

"Yes, Adam, I will marry you."

A big smile lit his face. "I thought you were going to say no."

"I'm sorry for the tears. I don't know why I cried. I'm not a crier, really I'm not." She swiped at her face with a mitten-covered hand. "I love you so much, Adam."

"When do you think we can get married?"

"Not until spring." She gave him a final hug. "I have so much to do. I have to make my dress. And a hope chest. I must have a hope chest. I had one—Mama and I started working on it when I was about ten years old—but it was lost in the fire." A shadow crossed her face. "I wish you could have met Mama and Papa, Adam. They would have loved you almost as much as I do."

"I'm sure I would have loved them; after all, they raised the most wonderful young lady. I thought maybe next week would be a good time."

"To get married?" Emily laughed. "Oh, my! That's much too soon. I have to finish out the school year."

"You don't have a contract."

"No, but I do have an obligation. Besides, there are all those other things to be taken care of. The dress and—"

"The hope chest." Adam laughed. "All right, I give up. School ends the middle of April. How about the following Saturday?"

"I was thinking maybe June would be a good time."

"June? That's too far away. How about May?"

"Ruth's baby is due in April. I want to be sure she's able to come." Emily considered for a moment. "The second Sunday in May. We can have the ceremony after church."

"Sounds good to me." Adam pulled her close and kissed her. "Now I think I had better take you home."

Emily's head whirled with one idea after another as she thought of the months ahead. She scarcely noticed when he picked up the lines and urged the horses forward. There was so much to do. So many plans to be made. "I can hardly wait to tell Sarah." She clasped her hands and her green eyes sparkled. "And Mrs. Sloan. They will be so surprised. Oh, Adam, I'm so happy, I can hardly contain myself. I feel like singing." And sitting beside Adam on the high wagon seat, she did that very thing.

seventeen

With Sarah and Mrs. Sloan's help, Emily began to work on her hope chest. After supper, they all took up needle and thread and embroidered pillowcases and tea towels. Mrs. Sloan's shuttle flew as she tatted lace edgings for the pillowcases. Crochet hooks transformed white thread into ruffled doilies. The three women talked and laughed as they worked.

In December, Michael proposed to Sarah, and a few items were added to her overflowing hope chest. In January, another three-day blizzard confined them to the house, and they began to work on wedding dresses. Sarah's wedding would be the end of April, so they made her dress first.

Saturday evenings, when the weather allowed, Adam came to town. The two young couples met at the Sloans'. They played games, made fudge, and popped corn.

Occasionally, Adam brought the wagon and they all rode out to the Thompsons'. The brothers would bring out their fiddle and banjo, and accompanied by Adam's guitar, they would all sing. To Emily's surprise, Bertha had a beautiful soprano singing voice, and Lewis sang a tolerable bass. Everyone else ranged somewhere in between.

Kirsten and Bertha were both expecting in the early spring. Kirsten confided one evening when the four women were alone in the kitchen that she was terrified of childbirth. "Scared spitless," as she expressed it.

"Land sakes!" Bertha exclaimed. "You ain't got nothin' to be afraid of."

"My mother died when I was born," Kirsten said. "I don't

want to die and leave my baby to be raised by strangers like I was."

"You was raised by your aunt—your mother's own sister— she wasn't no stranger."

"Well, she was to me," Kirsten exclaimed.

"Ever'body was a stranger to you," Bertha snapped. "Seein' as how you was a newborn baby."

Emily stood at the kitchen range, moving the covered skillet over the heat. Her shoulders shook with barely suppressed mirth.

Sarah clamped her hand over her mouth to smother a giggle, but it came out her nose in the form of a snort.

"I wasn't a baby when I left there," Kirsten retorted, "but I was still a stranger. Auntie reminded me every day of my life that I was a burden to her. I don't want that to happen to my baby. I want my baby to be loved."

"Your baby will be loved no matter what happens to you." Bertha set a bowl down for Emily's first skillet full of popped corn. "But there ain't nothin' gonna happen. I birthed Tad without an ounce of trouble, and he weighed almost nine pounds. Ma gave birth to five and never uttered a sound. And she was narrow-hipped like me. As broad as you are through the hips, you oughtn't to have a lick of trouble."

Emily shook the skillet and listened as the kernels of corn exploded against the lid. Sarah stood beside her, shaking salt on the popcorn in the bowl. She nudged Emily with her elbow and mouthed the words *pioneer women*.

Bertha put her hands on her slender hips and glared at her young sister-in-law. "Pioneer women had their babies in covered wagons alongside the trail, attended only by the other women, and they never uttered a single complaint. The wagon train never even slowed down. When my pa wanted to go west, my ma left all she held dear and followed him—even if she was in the family way. Pioneer women do what they have to do, and they don't never fuss and whine about it, neither."

Sarah grinned an "I-told-you-so" at Emily and sprinkled salt on the latest pan of popcorn.

Kirsten's hands clenched at her sides. "I am not a pioneer woman, Bertha. And neither are you. As far as I know, you have never been in a covered wagon in your life, and I am sick of hearing about pioneer women. Maybe they did have their babies in covered wagons. But they died like flies having them. And I don't want to die." She put her hand to her stomach. "This baby is the first thing I have ever had that belonged to me. I love my baby, and I want to raise him myself. I do not want my baby raised by a stranger."

Emily didn't know what Bertha would say, but she knew Bertha's tongue was razor sharp. "I think we have plenty of popcorn, Bertha," she said. "Shall we join the men?"

To Emily's astonishment, Bertha hugged her sister-in-law. "I know you're scared, Kirsten. I was, too. But everything will be all right. I'll be with you ever' step of the way, and Doc Brown will be here to take care of you. You will live to hold your grandchildren in your arms." She cleared her throat. "I'm sorry for bein' so short with you."

Kirsten forgave Bertha, and the four women joined the men in the parlor. Later, in the privacy of Sarah's bedroom, Sarah and Emily discussed the evening.

"I never would have believed it if I hadn't seen it," Sarah remarked. "But the pioneer woman has a heart after all."

"Sarah, you shouldn't call her that," Emily scolded.

"You are probably right. But Bertha would be flattered." Sarah adjusted a pillow behind her head and settled back on her bed. "Poor Kirsten is really frightened of childbirth."

"Her mother did die." Emily sat on the edge of the bed

beside Sarah. "I can understand her being frightened."

"Are you afraid, Emily?"

"I always hoped that when I married, I would have a houseful of children. I hadn't really thought about the dangers of giving birth before." Emily's face became thoughtful. "I still want children, though. What about you?"

"Michael and I want a large family." Sarah sighed. "I guess my biggest fear is that I'll never be able to have children of my own. Two of Mama's sisters never had children. Aunt Bethene had one, but I suppose one like Trudy was more than enough. Mama had Ben and me. We aren't a very prolific family."

Emily patted Sarah's arm. "You'll probably have a dozen."

"Michael says if we can't have our own, we'll raise someone else's."

"You mean you will adopt?"

"Mm-hmm. I'd like to have a couple of our own, though. But even if we do, we'll still adopt." She pushed herself into a sitting position. "We will probably always be poor as church mice, but our house will be filled with love."

The girls chatted for a few more minutes before Emily went to her own room. Lying in her bed that night, Emily thought about the children she hoped to have. Would they look like her? Or would they look like Adam? Maybe they would be a combination of the two of them. She fell asleep with a prayer on her lips for the children who would someday be given into her care.

⁂

There were two more blizzards before the days began to grow longer. Emily's and Sarah's days were spent planning their weddings and collecting donations of money and books for the new school library.

Charles Wise's visits to the community church continued, though as time passed, his attendance became less furtive.

Emily, Sarah, and Michael continued to pray for him.

Early in April, Mr. Sloan brought home a copy of the *Cleveland Press*. "A friend of mine sent me this paper," he commented as he handed it to Emily. "This wasn't where you worked by any chance, was it?"

Emily glanced at the paper, then read the first few paragraphs of the news story. "At 4:45 p.m. on Saturday, March 25, as the girls were preparing to go home, the Triangle Shirtwaist Company erupted in flames. In less than thirty minutes, 146 people, mostly young women, were dead."

"It can't be," Emily murmured. But she knew it was. Casting the newspaper aside, she huddled in the corner of the couch. "I can't believe they are all dead."

"Oh, Emily!" Sarah sat beside her and held her hand. "Did you know them? Were they your friends?"

"I don't know." Emily shook her head. "I might have known them. I worked on the ninth floor, but I never made friends. We were there to work, not to socialize."

"It could have been you," Sarah said. "You could have been one of the girls trapped by the fire."

That evening, Adam and Emily went for a ride in the country, and she told him about the fire. "It could have been you," Adam repeated Sarah's comment as he drew Emily into his arms.

She rested her head against his shoulder. "A few months before I came to work there, the girls went on strike. All they asked, Adam, was for sanitary workrooms and more safety precautions in the shop."

"They didn't get what they asked for?"

"No, and now they're dead." She snuggled closer. "We were never allowed to use the front door. We always went one at a time out the back door. There was a man there searching each of us because they were afraid we would take something. That door was always locked. The other doors opened inward.

There was only one fire escape. They could never have gotten out."

That night, the dreams that had haunted Emily's nights after her parents' deaths returned. This time many girls—their streaming hair ablaze—hurtled through the flames. She never saw or heard their bodies collide with the pavement. She jerked awake before she heard the impact the newspaper reporter described so vividly.

❧

Within the next three days, a trio of babies was born. Kirsten's healthy baby boy came first, followed closely by Bertha's daughter. Last of all, Ruth gave birth to a beautiful baby girl. The day after her birth, Adam made the trip into town to tell Emily.

"Ruth thought you might want to come meet her new daughter." He grinned down at her from the wagon seat when she came out of school.

"Of course I do." Emily turned to Sarah. "You don't mind, do you? I won't stay long."

Sarah made shooing motions with her hand. "Go on. Of course I don't mind. Give mother and daughter my love."

Adam jumped from the wagon to help Emily climb aboard, and soon they were on their way.

Later, as she held the soft bundle in her arms, breathing in that special newborn scent, Emily put the thought of death and her recent nightmare behind her and embraced the newness of life.

"She's beautiful, Ruth."

The smile hadn't left Ruth's face since Emily stepped into the bedroom, where she sat with her baby held close. "Her name is Emily Ruth."

Emily choked up but managed to say, "Oh, Ruth, you didn't have to do that."

Ruth's smile widened. "I know. I wanted to. I think it's a beautiful name."

"I don't know what to say except thank you." Emily studied the tiny features of the baby. Soft blond hair framed her face as she slept.

Strange new feelings stirred within Emily's heart. She looked up at Ruth. "I hope that someday God gives me a baby just as precious as this one."

"He will."

eighteen

The Saturday following little Emily Ruth's birth, the box social to raise money for the library was on the calendar. School would be dismissed for the summer the following Wednesday.

When Emily and Sarah came home from school Friday afternoon, a young woman with red hair sat at the kitchen table watching Mrs. Sloan prepare supper. She stood when they entered the kitchen and embraced Sarah.

"Sarah, darling, it's so good to see you."

Even before Sarah turned to Emily with a stricken look, she knew who the visitor was. "Emily, this is my cousin, Gertrude Phillips."

"Trudy, please, Sarah," the young woman admonished.

"I'm pleased to meet you, Miss Phillips." As Emily extended her hand, she felt her heart shattering.

Gertrude ignored her outstretched hand, looking down her nose at her instead. "Who might your little friend be, Sarah?"

"This is Emily Foster." Mrs. Sloan turned from the stove to answer for her daughter. "She teaches with Sarah. Emily is our boarder, but we think of her as a daughter."

"Indeed!" Gertrude's eyes narrowed. "How long have you been in Sanctuary, Miss Foster?"

"Since October," Emily managed to reply around the lump in her throat.

Mrs. Sloan wiped her hands on a dish towel. "Emily and Adam Jacobs are to be married in May."

"I see."

Emily felt a chill as Gertrude's blue eyes moved from her hair down to her shoes then traveled slowly back to her face.

"Excuse me," Emily murmured. "I have to change my clothes."

Alone in her room with the door closed, she threw herself across the bed. Sarah's cousin had a hard look that aged her beyond the twenty-three years Emily knew her to be. Her clothes were flashy and cheap looking. She saw nothing attractive in the woman's appearance. But Adam had loved her.

Why did she have to come back?

She rolled onto her back and lay looking up at the ceiling. Closing her eyes, she tried to visualize Gertrude and Adam—her Adam—together. She couldn't. It was impossible. Still, he had mourned that woman for a year. Her heart felt as a heavy stone. Maybe he had only turned to her because he thought Gertrude was unattainable. Maybe now that she had returned. . .

Emily allowed her doubts to run rampant for a short time. Then she did what she had advised Sarah to do. She took her burden to the throne, laid it at her Savior's feet, and left it there.

A few minutes later, when Sarah knocked on her door, Emily was able to greet her with a smile.

"I was afraid you were in here crying your eyes out," Sarah said as soon as the door closed behind her.

"Believe me, I thought about it." Emily settled on the vanity stool. "But I knew tears would be a waste of time. Instead of crying, I decided to follow my own advice."

Sarah perched on the edge of the bed. "You left it with the Lord?"

"I did."

"She's pretty awful, isn't she?"

Emily pleated her skirt between her fingers. "I don't know her well enough to make that judgment."

"Well, believe me, I do." Sarah wrinkled her nose. "Gertrude was on her best behavior today. If Mama hadn't been there, she would have shown her true colors."

"I don't wish to speak ill of your cousin." Emily smoothed the pleats from her skirt. "It is only that she isn't at all what I expected."

"I told you what she was like, Emily."

"I know you did. But Adam loved her."

"She's deceitful. Adam never saw the real Gertrude." Sarah reached across the space that separated them to clasp Emily's hand. "I've told you that before."

"I think it is a blessing she came back. If Adam still has feelings for her, I would much rather find out now than after we are married."

"Adam never loved her," Sarah scoffed.

That was what Adam had told Emily, and she had believed him, but now, despite her prayers, a seed of doubt had been planted in her heart. "Well, I guess only time will tell. It's in the Lord's hands now, and I think we shouldn't discuss it any further." Emily feared that any more discussion would send her back to the altar to pick up the burden she knew she could not carry. She stood. "I should imagine your mother could use help with supper."

"It's for sure Trudy won't lift a hand to—" At Emily's warning glance, Sarah changed the subject. "We have to decide what we are going to prepare for the box social." She followed Emily out the door. "I wish it were July."

"Are you that eager to be an old married lady?" Emily teased.

"After waiting all these years, you had better believe I am." Sarah laughed. "I was actually thinking of making fried chicken, but I don't think the first fryers will be ready until Independence Day. Just think, Emily, by the Fourth of July, we will both have surrendered our independence."

Sitting at the dining room table, Gertrude said nothing about where she had been the last year. Nor did she offer a hint of what she had been doing. As soon as supper was over, she pled exhaustion and retired to the room she would share with Sarah.

"That's Gertrude for you," Sarah said, her hands immersed in hot, soapy dishwater. "She doesn't do dishes."

"I am sure she is tired." Emily lifted a plate from the steaming rinse water.

"She's always tired when there is work to be done." Sarah wrinkled her nose. "You are certainly charitable."

"Not as much as I should be." Emily added the dried plate to the stack on the counter. "What do you think she is doing here?"

"She's up to no good, that's for certain." Sarah slid a bowl into the rinse water. "I wonder what happened to the magnificent Vito."

"Gertrude's sweetheart was Italian?"

"So he said, but I doubt that was his real name. Vito and Trudy were a delightful couple. They deserved one another." Sarah sighed. "It's my guess he abandoned her and she had nowhere else to go."

"How long do you think she will be here?"

"Until she gets what she came for." She put a soapy hand on Emily's wrist. "Maybe we should keep Michael and Adam hidden until she is gone."

Emily laughed. "No one could come between you and Michael." Her face grew serious. "If Adam truly loves me, as he says he does, nothing Gertrude can do will change that."

"It's just that she is so conniving." Sarah scrubbed furiously on a pan. "There is nothing she won't do to get what she wants."

"I think she is hurting."

"She deserves to hurt after the havoc she created last time she was here," Sarah grumbled.

"We should pray for her. Gertrude is a fallen sparrow, Sarah. She needs help. Divine help."

"You know what I think?" Sarah slid the pan into the rinse water. "I believe you are a candidate for sainthood, Emily."

"You wouldn't think so if you could read my thoughts." Emily lifted the stack of clean plates into the cabinet. "I would like to scream and throw things and tell your cousin that Adam is mine. Then I would like to chase that painted floozy out of town before he ever catches sight of her."

Sarah giggled. "My goodness! You are human after all."

"All too human, I fear." Emily sighed. "What I am going to do is ask for grace. Then I'm going to pray for Gertrude Phillips."

That night alone in her bedroom, Emily prayed for Gertrude. She prayed for Adam. She prayed for herself. Last of all, she prayed that she might have the strength to accept God's will. "And whatever happens," she prayed, "help me to accept it and grow closer to You, Lord."

Her prayer completed, she crawled into bed and slept soundly until the first rays of sun crept through her window.

It was almost noon on Saturday before Gertrude wandered into the kitchen, where Emily and Sarah were rolling out piecrusts. Her uncombed red hair straggled around her face and onto the neck of her scarlet dressing gown. Her face, scrubbed free of makeup, looked unnaturally pale. She slumped into a chair at the table and demanded, "Sarah, bring me a cup of coffee!"

Sarah rolled her eyes as she filled a cup from the pot on the back of the stove then set it in front of her cousin. "This is probably strong enough to remove paint. Breakfast was hours ago."

"I'm sorry I didn't make it, but I'd forgotten how dreadfully early you people get up." Gertrude covered a yawn. "Where's Aunt Molly?"

"Mama is helping Papa at the paper." Sarah slapped some dough on the breadboard and began to roll it out while Emily filled the crust she had just completed.

"Uncle Henry still operates that quaint little newspaper?" Gertrude studied Emily over the rim of her coffee cup. "What kind of pies are you making?"

Although she looked at Emily, Sarah answered. "We have dried apple in the oven. These are raisin. Emily is making them. Adam thinks her raisin pies are the absolute best he's ever eaten."

If Sarah had wanted a reaction from Gertrude, she didn't get it. "Well, aren't you the industrious little homemakers?" She didn't bother to stifle her yawn this time. "Are you getting ready for a pie supper or something?"

"Maybe we just enjoy baking." Sarah didn't bother hiding the sarcasm in her voice.

"We are having a box social tonight at the school. We'll fix the rest of the meal later." Emily spoke for the first time.

"Oh, really!" Gertrude's eyes sparked with interest. "Will everybody be going?"

"It's a fund-raiser for our new school library." Emily crimped the edges of the piecrust. "We are expecting a large turnout."

"Then I suppose that means I may go."

Sarah and Emily exchanged glances. Emily wanted to say, "No, you are too late!" Instead, she said, "Of course you may." She managed a smile. "We would be happy to have you."

"As soon as I get dressed, I'll help you bake." Gertrude pushed back her chair. "You do have something I can put my supper in, don't you?"

Without waiting for an answer, Gertrude sauntered from the room.

"I suppose you know she isn't going to help," Sarah muttered as soon as her cousin was out of earshot. "You shouldn't have told her what we were doing."

"She would have found out anyway." Emily slipped a raisin pie into the oven. "We couldn't leave her here alone."

"I suppose not." Sarah sighed. "She would probably steal the family silver."

"That's a terrible thing to say."

"I know. I apologize." Sarah snickered. "But it's true."

"Is she always that pale?" Emily frowned. "I thought she looked ill."

"She is a bit peaked, and those dark circles under her eyes made her look even paler." Sarah dried her hands on the dish towel. "I overheard Mama tell Papa she thinks Gertrude is"—Sarah blushed, and her voice dropped to a whisper—"in the family way."

"Oh, no! Surely not."

"I wouldn't be surprised if Mama is right." Sarah hung the dish towel up to dry. "It would be just like Gertrude to get herself into trouble then come running back to Sanctuary. You know what probably happened, Emily?"

"She married her sweetheart after she left Sanctuary," Emily said, grasping at straws. "He will be joining her soon."

"No." Sarah shook her head. "I think when he found out she was—you know—he abandoned her. She couldn't go home, so she came here."

"Why would she come to Sanctuary?"

"I'm not sure, but knowing Gertrude, she has some nefarious scheme brewing." Sarah patted Emily's arm. "Keep an eye on her, and don't trust her. Trudy will stop at nothing to get what she wants."

Almost an hour later, Gertrude made her way back to the kitchen. She had twisted her hair into an untidy bun on top of her head and put on a faded cotton housedress that pulled tight across her rather formidable bosom. With her face scrubbed clean, she gave the appearance of a slatternly but respectable housewife. She flitted around the kitchen getting in the way for the next half hour before sitting back down at the table.

"Start a new pot of coffee, Sarah."

"If you want a pot of coffee, start it yourself." Sarah's cheeks flushed. "We're busy."

Emily realized her friend was at the boiling point. Hoping to avoid an unpleasant confrontation, she started the pot of coffee. "It will be ready in a few minutes. In the meantime, would you like something to eat?"

Gertrude's gaze came to rest on the four loaves of bread Sarah had just turned out on the breadboard. "You might fix me a slice of bread and butter. Oh, and if you have any of Aunt Molly's plum preserves, they would go nicely."

Aware of Sarah's disapproving glare, Emily prepared Gertrude's breakfast. She placed it, along with a fresh cup of coffee, in front of her before returning to the mountain of dirty dishes piled in the sink.

"So you are planning to marry Adam Jacobs." Gertrude's statement stilled Emily's hands in the hot dishwater.

"Adam and Emily are to be married in May," Sarah answered for her. "I am marrying Michael Barnes. Emily is marrying Adam." Sarah rested the palms of her hands on the table and leaned toward her cousin. "What are you doing here, Gertrude? Why did you come back?"

Emily detected a slight quiver of the redhead's lip, then she laughed. "It's Trudy. How many times must I tell you? I wanted to see my loved ones and mend a few fences." Her gaze moved to Emily. "How is Adam, Miss Foster? You know, we were betrothed. I made a terrible mistake when I left Adam. Now I have returned to make amends."

"You stay away from Adam, Gertrude." Sarah leaned closer. "I mean it."

Emily dried her hands and came to stand beside her friend. She put a hand on Sarah's shoulder. "It's all right. Gertrude and Adam were friends. Of course she will want to see him." Then, although the words tasted bitter on her tongue, she added, "And I'm sure Adam will want to see her."

nineteen

A short time later, after ordering Sarah to pack her supper for her, Gertrude went to her room. When she finally emerged, she was wearing a red dress and a matching hat with a long, curling feather. The dress was cut modestly enough to be acceptable in New York City perhaps, but not in Sanctuary, Montana. She had freshened her makeup and taken a curling iron to her flaming red hair. Emily thought she looked beautiful—in an overblown, garish way.

The girls put their names inside their identical baskets, then tied ribbons to match the color of their dresses around the handles. Blue for Sarah. Green for Emily. Red for Gertrude.

They walked the short distance to the school with Gertrude complaining every step of the way. "I thought Adam and Michael would pick you up," she grumbled.

"They would have," Sarah said. "But we had to be there early, so we told them to meet us at the school."

"I don't see why you had to go so early."

"I told you," Sarah replied. "We are in charge of the social. We have things to do."

"Someone else could have done it." Gertrude stumbled over a loose stone in the road and uttered an expletive that caused both Emily and Sarah to blush. "Now I've twisted my ankle. And besides, I'm cold."

"I told you to wait and ride over with Mama and Daddy." Sarah increased her pace. "You chose to walk with us, so stop complaining."

Emily was accustomed to walking and had no problem

keeping up with Sarah. Gertrude, however, lagged a step behind and was so short of breath, she couldn't talk.

When they arrived in the large assembly hall of the school, they deposited their baskets on a long table at the front of the room. While Sarah and Emily arranged tables and chairs, Gertrude hovered around their baskets. When people began to arrive and other boxes and baskets joined the three on the table, she moved to the sidelines and sat down.

By the time Adam walked through the door, a good-sized crowd had gathered. He saw Emily immediately and crossed the room to take her hand in his.

"Hi." He smiled down at her.

"Hi, yourself." She forced a smile.

"What's wrong?" Before she had a chance to reply, a hand with long red fingernails clutched his forearm.

"Adam, darling. I've been watching for you."

For a moment, he didn't recognize the woman clinging to him. He stared at her and then pulled his arm free. "Trudy, what are you doing here?"

She laughed. "Why, I came to see you, darling. Why else would I return to Sanctuary?"

Adam put his arm around Emily and drew her close to his side. "Emily and I are to be married in May. Surely you know that."

"Of course. Congratulations, Adam. I hope you will be very happy." Her blue-eyed gaze shifted to the door. "Aunt Molly and Uncle Henry are here now. If you will excuse me."

Emily watched Gertrude make her way to her aunt and uncle. Adam's arm tightened around her shoulders, assuring her of his love. She put the other woman out of her mind and smiled up at him.

Matt Reed made a short speech. Then Michael prayed before he announced the beginning of the bidding. When

Adam asked which dinner was hers, Emily pointed out the basket on the end with the green ribbon tied around the handle.

There was a lot of good-natured teasing and laughter as the dinners were auctioned off. Finally, Mr. Reed held up the basket with the green ribbon. "What am I offered for this basket?" He raised the corner of the white linen napkin and sniffed. "Something in here smells mighty appetizing."

Several of Adam's friends bid on the basket, dropping out one by one, until Adam gave the final bid of five dollars.

"Adam, if you will come forward to claim your basket and the young lady who prepared it." Mr. Reed removed the small card from the basket. He looked at the name, then adjusted his glasses and looked again. "Miss Trudy Phillips?"

The buzz of voices lowered to a murmur.

"How did this happen?" Adam looked down into Emily's pale face. "I will not eat with her."

The memory of Gertrude hovering around the table that held their three baskets flashed through Emily's mind. The devious woman had switched the ribbons or the names while Emily and Sarah were setting up tables. Emily's heart plunged. "It's all right, Adam. I know what happened. Go ahead and eat with her. I'll explain later."

&

Adam didn't want to share a meal with Trudy, but in order to avoid a scene, he picked up the basket and allowed the beaming redhead to lead him to a table. He felt even worse when Charles Wise had the successful bid on the basket with the red ribbon. The basket that belonged to Emily.

"Adam, darling, I'm so glad you bought my basket." Trudy chattered as she unpacked the basket. "I even made raisin pie, your favorite."

Adam looked at the piece of pie in Gertrude's hand. "You didn't make that pie. Emily did. And another thing. Do not call me 'darling.'"

"I'm sorry." When he sat down without pulling her chair out for her, she seated herself in the chair across the table from him. "I realize you have every right to be angry with me. I'm sorry for the things I said in that letter. You must know I didn't mean any of them."

Adam's attention was across the room, where Emily and Charles Wise were immersed in discussion. "What letter?"

"The letter I left with Sarah to give to—" The color rose in her face. "Never mind." Her gaze followed his. "It looks as though your little sweetheart is enjoying herself."

Adam looked at Trudy. How could he have ever imagined himself to be in love with her? Everything about her repulsed him. "Emily is pure gold."

"How sweet." Trudy's shrill laugh grated on his ears like chalk on a blackboard. Had she always been this cheap and common?

"I realized what a terrible mistake I had made leaving you, but by then it was too late. Vito turned out to be a monster." She brushed away a tear while her lower lip pouted. "He was cruel, Adam. He beat me."

Adam watched two matching tears trickle down her face. Crocodile tears, he realized now. Trudy had always been able to weep at will. Why had he been so easily fooled by this woman? There wasn't a sincere bone in her entire body. He saw her red lips moving, but he didn't listen. He turned his gaze to Emily. And couldn't find her. Charles Wise also had disappeared. He quickly scanned the room but could find neither of them.

&

"I've been wanting to talk to you, Miss Foster." Emily slid

into the chair Charles held for her. He sat down across from her. "I need to apologize for my boorish behavior last fall."

"That is quite all right, Mr. Wise." Her gaze crossed the room to Adam.

Charles looked over his shoulder at the other couple. "Mr. Jacobs appears quite miserable, doesn't he?"

Adam did look miserable. Emily smiled. "Yes, he does."

"Whatever possessed him to buy that woman's basket?"

"I don't believe he intended to."

Charles turned back to Emily. "I'm glad that he did. I've been wanting to talk to you, but school didn't seem the proper place. I have a confession to make, Miss Foster. I have been a fool."

Emily focused her attention on Charles. "I am listening, Mr. Wise."

"I was raised in a Bible-believing home," Charles began. He proceeded to tell Emily about his family and their faith. When he went away to college, his mother had tucked a Bible in with his other belongings, but he never bothered to read it. Away from his parents' influence, Charles fell in with a group of evolutionists and eventually embraced their philosophy.

"Charles Darwin was a great scientist, a learned man; surely he knew more than my parents. At least that's what I told myself. I felt so proud to bear the same given name. Then I came to Sanctuary." He looked down at the untouched food on his plate. "And I met you. You are very like my mother, Miss Foster." He looked into Emily's eyes. "I started reading the Bible my mother gave me, and after attending your church, I determined to gather my facts and present them to you. I planned to refute everything you believe. Instead, I find it is I who was wrong. There is only one God. Creator of the universe. Giver of life."

"Then you have accepted Christ, Mr. Wise?"

"In my head, yes." Charles placed a hand over his heart. "In here, not yet."

"Would you like me to pray with you, Mr. Wise?" Emily leaned forward.

"I feel so unworthy."

"Yes, you are," Emily agreed. "We all are. But the Father understands and He forgives. Do you know John 3:16, Mr. Wise?"

" 'For God so loved the world, that he gave his only begotten Son, that whosoever believeth in him should not perish, but have everlasting life.' I was probably four years old when I memorized that verse."

"I can't even imagine such love, Mr. Wise." Emily's face shone. "But I do know if Emily Foster had been the only person on earth—or if Charles Wise had been—God would still have sent His Son to die for me or for you. If you are ready to ask Jesus into your heart, I will pray with you."

"I'm ready, Miss Foster." Charles glanced around the room. "But not here. Perhaps we could go to one of the classrooms."

"That would be fine." Emily stood.

"Just a moment. I would like to ask Michael and Miss Sloan to accompany us." Charles glanced around the room.

Michael and Sarah were sitting a few tables away. When Charles spoke to them, they immediately pushed their supper to one side. The four young people left the room together.

❧

"What's wrong, Adam? Did you lose something?" Gertrude smiled. "Or someone?"

"Everything is fine, Trudy." Adam forced his gaze back to Trudy. The self-satisfied expression on her face sickened him.

"I was wrong to leave you, Adam." Gertrude rested her

hand on his. "Can you ever forgive me?"

"I forgive you, Trudy." Adam slid his hand from beneath hers. "I should thank you for leaving."

"You don't mean that, darling." Trudy's full red lips pouted. "You're just upset because your little sweetheart took off with that little twit she was so engrossed with."

"Trudy, you wouldn't understand a woman like Emily." He pushed aside his plate. "I thank God every day for bringing her into my life."

"I'm in trouble, Adam." Her lower lip trembled. "I need you."

"I'm sorry, Trudy, but your trouble has nothing to do with me." He folded his napkin and laid it beside his plate. Over her shoulder, he saw Emily, Charles, Michael, and Sarah enter the room. "Now I will bid you good evening and good-bye."

He pushed back his chair and stood. As soon as Emily saw him, she left Sarah and the two men and crossed the room to him.

"Oh, Adam, you'll never believe what just now happened." A radiant smile lit up her face. "Mr. Wise gave his heart to Jesus. Isn't that wonderful?"

"That is wonderful." His love for her was so strong, it took his breath away. "You are wonderful. I knew I loved you, but until tonight I never realized how much."

Then, with half the town watching, Adam Jacobs took his mail-order bride into his arms and kissed her with such heartfelt love that no one noticed when Gertrude Phillips stomped from the room amid the thundering applause and catcalls.

A Letter To Our Readers

Dear Reader:

In order that we might better contribute to your reading enjoyment, we would appreciate your taking a few minutes to respond to the following questions. We welcome your comments and read each form and letter we receive. When completed, please return to the following:

Fiction Editor
Heartsong Presents
PO Box 719
Uhrichsville, Ohio 44683

1. Did you enjoy reading *Escape to Sanctuary* by M. J. Conner?
   ❑ Very much! I would like to see more books by this author!
   ❑ Moderately. I would have enjoyed it more if

   _____

   _____

   _____

2. Are you a member of **Heartsong Presents**? ❑ Yes ❑ No
   If no, where did you purchase this book? _____

   _____

3. How would you rate, on a scale from 1 (poor) to 5 (superior), the cover design? _____

4. On a scale from 1 (poor) to 10 (superior), please rate the following elements.

   ____ Heroine   ____ Plot
   ____ Hero   ____ Inspirational theme
   ____ Setting   ____ Secondary characters

5. These characters were special because?_____
_____
_____

6. How has this book inspired your life?_____
_____
_____

7. What settings would you like to see covered in future
   Heartsong Presents books?_____
_____
_____

8. What are some inspirational themes you would like to see
   treated in future books?_____
_____
_____

9. Would you be interested in reading other **Heartsong
   Presents** titles? ❑ Yes ❑ No

10. Please check your age range:
       ❑ Under 18   ❑ 18-24
       ❑ 25-34   ❑ 35-45
       ❑ 46-55   ❑ Over 55

Name_____
Occupation _____
Address _____

BRIDES O' THE
Emerald Isle

4 stories in 1

When the little town of Ballymara's tourism is threatened by a cynical journalist, Moyra Rose O'Cullen challenges him. Tracing history back in time, she uncovers the roots of the local legend of the pledging stone at the door to the chapel and learns three stories of how her ancestors' bonds of love were formed over the ancient stone.

Authors include Pamela Griffen, Vickie McDonough, Tamela Hancock Murray, and Linda Windsor.

Historical, paperback, 352 pages, 5 ³/₁₆" x 8"

Presents

Great Inspirational Romance at a Great Price!

Heartsong Presents books are inspirational romances in contemporary and historical settings, designed to give you an enjoyable, spirit-lifting reading experience. You can choose wonderfully written titles from some of today's best authors like Peggy Darty, Sally Laity, DiAnn Mills, Colleen L. Reece, Debra White Smith, and many others.

When ordering quantities less than twelve, above titles are $2.97 each.
Not all titles may be available at time of order.